D0464777

love in lowercase

Center Point
Large Print

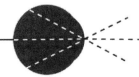

**This Large Print Book carries the
Seal of Approval of N.A.V.H.**

love in lowercase

Francesc Miralles

Translated by Julie Wark

CENTER POINT LARGE PRINT
THORNDIKE, MAINE

This Center Point Large Print edition is published in
the year 2016 by arrangement with Penguin Books,
an imprint of Penguin Publishing Group,
a division of Penguin Random House LLC.

First published in Great Britain under the title *Love in Small
Letters* by Alma Books Limited 2014. Originally published in
Spanish as *Amor en minuscula* by Amsterdam Llibres, an imprint
of Ara Llibres SCCL in 2010. This translation, based on a revised
text, published by Alma Books Limited in 2014.

Excerpt from "Prayer for Marilyn Monroe"
from *Pluriverse: New and Selected Poems* by
Ernesto Cardenal. Copyright © 1977 by Ernesto Cardenal.
Translation copyright © 1977, 1980 by Robert Pring-Mill.
Used by permission of New Directions Publishing Corp.

The text of this Large Print edition is unabridged. In other
aspects, this book may vary from the original edition.
Printed in the United States of America on permanent paper.
Set in 16-point Times New Roman type.

ISBN: 978-1-62899-904-4

Library of Congress Cataloging-in-Publication Data

Names: Miralles, Francesc, 1968– author. | Wark, Julie, translator.
Title: Love in lowercase / Francesc Miralles ; translated by Julie Wark.
Other titles: Amor en minúscula. English
Description: Center Point Large Print edition. | Thorndike, Maine : Center Point
Large Print, 2016. | ©2014
Identifiers: LCCN 2015046461 | ISBN 9781628999044
    (hardcover : alk. paper)
Subjects: LCSH: Large type books.
Classification: LCC PC3942.423.I73 A8313 2016 | DDC 849/.916—dc23
LC record available at http://lccn.loc.gov/2015046461

In memory of
Julia Tappert

Enjoy the little things,
for one day you may look back
and realize they were the big things.

—ROBERT BRAULT

Contents

I

Sea of Fog

II

The Dark Side of the Moon

III
- - - -
The Pathos of Things

V

One Day in a Life

love in lowercase

I

Sea of Fog

650,000 Hours

In no time at all the year was going to end and the new one was about to begin. Human inventions for selling calendars. After all, we're the ones who've arbitrarily decided when the years, months, and even hours start. We shape the world in our own measure, and that soothes us. Under the apparent chaos, maybe there really is order in the universe. However, it certainly won't be our order.

I was putting a minibottle of cava and a dozen grapes on the table—one for each stroke of midnight, as is the custom in this country—and thinking about hours. I'd read somewhere that the battery of a human life runs down after 650,000 hours.

Considering the medical history of the males in my family, I calculated that my best life expectancy in terms of hours was lower than the average: 600,000 at most. At thirty-seven, I could very well be halfway through. The question was, how many thousands of hours had I wasted so far?

Until just before midnight on that 31st of December, my life hadn't exactly been an adventure.

The only member of my family was one sister I

rarely saw. My existence alternated between the Department of German Studies and Linguistics, where I am an assistant lecturer, and my dreary apartment.

Outside my literature classes, I had very little contact with other people. In my spare time, when I wasn't preparing for classes and correcting exams, I did the typical things a boring bachelor does: read and reread books, listen to classical music, watch the news, and so on. It was a routine in which the biggest thrill was the odd trip to the supermarket.

Sometimes, I gave myself a treat on weekends and went to the Verdi movie complex to see a foreign film. I came out as lonely as when I went in, but at least it was something to do at the end of the day. Then, tucked in bed, I read the information sheet the Verdi supplied about the film, listing the credits, quoting praise from the critics (never anything negative), and offering interviews with the director or actors.

None of this ever changed my opinion of the film. Then I switched off the light.

That was when a strange sensation took over, the idea that there was no guarantee I was going to wake up the next morning. Worse, I'd get even more anxious when I started calculating how many days or even weeks would go by before somebody realized I'd died.

I'd been brooding about this ever since I read in

some newspaper that a Japanese man had been found in his apartment three years after his death. Everything suggested that no one had missed him.

Anyway, going back to the grapes . . . While I was thinking about wasted hours, I counted out the twelve grapes and set them out on a plate, next to which I'd placed the champagne glas and the minibottle. I've never been much of a drinker.

Having turned on the TV and tuned in to one of those programs that link up with some famous clock or another, I opened the bottle six minutes before the chimes of midnight began to ring out. I didn't want the new year to catch me unawares. I think the festivities were in Puerta del Sol in Madrid. Behind the pair of beautiful, glamorous hosts, an excited crowd was popping champagne corks. Some people were singing or jumping, waving their arms in the air in the hope that the cameras would capture them.

When people are lonely, they amuse themselves in very strange ways.

Midnight finally came, and I observed the ritual by putting one grape into my mouth with each chime. As I took a mouthful of cava and tried to wash down the grapes that were clogging up my throat, I couldn't help feeling ridiculous about having fallen into the trap of tradition. Who said I had to take part in that routine?

I decided it was a waste of time, so I wiped my mouth with a napkin and turned off the TV.

I could hear loud laughter and fireworks on the street as I undressed and got ready for bed. *How childish they are.* I switched off the light on yet another day.

I had trouble getting to sleep that night. I usually sleep with earplugs and mask, so it wasn't because of the noise outside, which was considerable, since I live between two squares in the bustling neighborhood of Gràcia.

For the first time in that festive season I felt lonely and vulnerable. I wanted the whole Christmas farce to end—and the sooner the better. I had five quiet days ahead, so to speak. Then, on January 6th, the Epiphany and last day of the Christmas holidays, I was going to have lunch with my sister and her husband, who's been depressed ever since I've known him. They don't have children.

It'll be a nightmare. Thank heavens everything will be back to normal on January 7th.

Comforted by this, I could feel my eyelids closing. But would they open again?

I'm already in the new year. But there's nothing new about it. That was my last thought.

I went to sleep, not knowing how wrong I was.

A Saucer of Milk

I got up early with the feeling that the whole city, except for me, was asleep. The silence was so intense that, although I was still in my pajamas, I had the guilty feeling that I was committing a crime by making myself a slice of buttered toast when most human beings were still sleeping off their hangovers.

I didn't suspect that the new year had a surprise in store for me—a small surprise, but one with world-shattering consequences. The fluttering of a butterfly's wings can cause a cataclysm on the other side of the world. A hurricane was now roaring in to blow down the façade behind which I'd confined my life. There is no weatherman who can forecast this kind of cyclone.

I turned on the gas, made some coffee, and swallowed the last mouthful of toast. Then I started to plan my day while I got dressed, which is what I usually do. I feel lost if I don't program my day, even on holidays.

I didn't have much choice. One possibility was to correct the essays of the stragglers who'd handed in their work just before Christmas rather than on December 1st as I'd asked, in order to have time to correct them. I decided against it.

I thought I might watch part of the New Year's

concert, even though I'm not crazy about waltzes. In any case, I had a couple of hours before it began.

I washed my face with a generous splash of water. Then it was time to comb my hair. I immediately spotted a new gray hair, which must have appeared overnight. I was certain it hadn't been there the day before.

OK, I know gray hairs are a sign of wisdom. I pulled it out with some tweezers. *But I don't want people to know I'm so wise.*

Gray hairs depress me more than hair loss. After all, if a hair falls out, there's always the chance that it will grow again and maybe even stronger. However, if it goes gray, there's no use hoping it will go black again, at least not naturally. On the contrary, the most probable thing is that it will turn completely white.

Assailed by these gloomy thoughts, I went into the living room. Walking past the telephone, I glanced at it forlornly. It hadn't rung on New Year's Eve—and neither had it made a peep on Christmas Eve, or on the morning of Christmas Day. Nothing led me to believe that things might change on January 1st.

Then again, that wasn't so surprising. I hadn't phoned anyone either.

I sat on the couch thinking I'd dive back into a book by an American writer whom I'd found quite entertaining the last few days. I'd bought it on Amazon after seeing it mentioned in a novel. It's called *They Have a Word for It*, and it's an odd dictionary of expressions that exist in only one language.

According to its author, Howard Rheingold, finding the name for something means ensuring its existence. We think and behave in certain ways because we have words to underpin what we're doing. In this sense, words shape thoughts.

Some examples of these unique words are:

Baraka: in Arabic, spiritual energy that can be used for worldly ends.

Won: the Korean word for the reluctance to give up an illusion.

Razblyuto: in Russian, the feeling one has for someone she has loved but no longer loves.

Mokita: the Kiriwina word for the truth that everyone knows but no one ever utters.

The author also mentions the Spanish word *ocurrencia*. I would never have thought that this was untranslatable.

I saw that there were a lot of entries in German, since—as long as certain rules are respected—anyone can construct new words in this language. One example it gave was *Torschlusspanik* (literally, panic at the closing of a door), the dismay of a childless woman faced with the irreversible ticking of the biological clock.

From what I could see, Japanese was the

language with the most subtle nuances, with expressions like *Ah-un* for the tacit understanding between two friends, or my favorite one: *Mono no aware*, to denote the pathos of things.

As I was pondering that last entry, I realized that I'd been hearing a persistent noise for several minutes. It was a slow, steady crunching sound, as if some insect was gnawing its way through the door.

I turned off the music to get a clearer idea of where the aggravating sound was coming from. It stopped that very moment, as if the culprit realized it had been detected.

Shrugging it off, I went back to the couch and picked up the book, but before I could focus on the page the noise started again, much louder.

It can't be an insect—not a normal-sized one, at least.

I listened harder and, yes, it seemed that the rasping was coming from the door. I went over to it warily, wondering what kind of lunatic would scratch at someone's door. Then I remembered that there is a monstrous creature in Bantu mythology, the *palatyi*, which does exactly that.

Man or monster, whatever it was, if it wanted to rattle me, it was succeeding. In any case, it had heard my footsteps and, by the time I was standing there, facing the door, it was scratching at the wood even more frantically.

Spurred on by fear, I flung the door open, hoping to startle my enemy.

But no one was there.

To be more precise, there was no human being visible at eye level. Bewildered and staring at the empty landing, I felt something soft and warm coiling around my legs.

I instinctively jumped backward and then looked down to see what had been attacking my door. It was a cat, which greeted me with melodious meowing—a young cat, but bigger than a kitten: a tabby, like millions of other cats that run around and climb things in this world.

The cat tried to placate me by rubbing against my legs more energetically, weaving a series of horizontal eights or Möbius strips—the symbol of infinity.

"That's enough," I said, and nudged the cat away with my ankle, trying to ease it back onto the landing.

But it came back inside and stared at me defiantly.

Overcoming the feeling of revulsion I've always had for cats, I picked it up, fearing that it might try to claw at me, but it only uttered a high-pitched meow.

"Off you go now," I ordered, throwing it unceremoniously onto the landing.

No sooner had it landed than the nimble creature dashed back inside before I could close the door.

I was losing my patience.

For a moment, I considered chasing it out with a broom, which is what my late father would have done in such circumstances. Perhaps it was an act of insubordination from this side of the grave, or a scrap of leftover Christmas spirit, but in the end I decided to give it a saucer of milk so it could fill its belly and stop bothering me.

I thought the cat would follow me to the kitchen, but it chose to wait by the front door, watching me hopefully.

I poured some milk into the saucer and walked slowly back down the corridor, trying not to spill it. When I got to the door the cat wasn't there.

Gone.

Since I'd left the door slightly ajar, I assumed the cat, feeling ignored, had left. Cursing the animal for making me fetch milk for nothing, I put the saucer down and looked out onto the landing to see if I could spot it.

Not a trace.

It must have gone off to try its luck at the other apartments.

I'm a rational, pragmatic man, and I don't like whimsical behavior. I'd brought milk for the cat; therefore the cat had to drink it. I started calling it—Kitty, Kitty, Kitty—but it didn't appear.

Fed up with playing a role that was strange to me, I left the saucer on the landing and closed the door.

The Sorrows of Young Werther

Lunchtime and the afternoon went by without any more surprises. I kept dipping into the dictionary, looking for strange words. Then I watched part of the New Year's concert but, irritated by the cheesy images of young couples holding hands and watching the snow falling outside a window, I turned off the TV.

My conscience reminded me that I had to do a bit of work, in order to avoid the uncomfortable feeling that I was wasting my time. This meant I had to get down to correcting the essays of my laggard students.

I'd given them an easy assignment: they had to write a two-page summary of Goethe's most popular novel, *Die Leiden des jungen Werthers*. The title has been translated as *The Sufferings of Young Werther* and *The Sorrows of Young Werther*. I preferred the latter version, perhaps because that was the one I'd owned before reading it in German.

The story, written in epistolary form, is well known. Young Werther moves to the idyllic village of Wahlheim, where he intends to enjoy a peaceful life of reading and painting. However, at a ball organized by the local youth, he meets

Charlotte—Lotte to her friends—and falls madly in love with her. Although Lotte is engaged to another man, Werther visits her frequently in the hope that she will return his love. His passion grows, as tends to happen when love is unrequited. Taking the advice of his friend and confidant Wilhelm, Werther leaves the village and takes a job as an ambassador's secretary. However, he can't stand the frivolity of his new life, so he returns to Wahlheim where, faced with the impossibility of loving the now married Lotte, he commits suicide by shooting himself.

Told like this, it might sound like a corny melodrama, but Goethe gives the whole story an existential feel. In the end, one has the impression that Werther's fervent love for Lotte is just an excuse, because the fact of the matter is that he's bored with life.

This, at least, is my interpretation. My students think differently. More than two centuries later, all of them, male and female, love the book. Perhaps it's because they're at an age when love can still be idealized.

My students like it when I tell them about the furor it caused in its day. In less than two years, it was translated into twelve languages, Chinese among them—an extraordinary thing at the time. The work inspired a particular way of being, which was taken up all around the world. Legions of romantics got dressed up in blue coats and yellow vests and, like Werther, wept copiously and wrote desperate letters to their beloveds. Even Napoleon claimed to have read the book seven times, and that he always had it with him on the battlefield.

Imitating their hero, hundreds of young men killed themselves, and in some cities—Leipzig, for example—the novel was banned.

Werther is largely responsible for the idea of romantic love that survives to this day. It is a magnificent work, even though some of Werther's antics are laughable. I suspect that Goethe himself had a little giggle as he was writing some of those lines.

The Assault

The freezing night had misted up the windows of my kitchen, where I was cooking dinner in silence. I've never liked the end of the day, because its waning seems to forebode my own decline. That is when loneliness bites most viciously with its invisible fangs.

As I cooked a potato omelet in my single-serving frying pan, I wondered why things had never worked out with any of my girlfriends. The last one was years ago. She was a lovely blonde, and her only problem was that she already had a boyfriend, although it took me months to discover that. In the end, her brother felt sorry for me and, taking me aside one day, advised me to bail out.

"She doesn't want to be with either of you," he warned. "If she loved her boyfriend, she wouldn't have gotten involved with you, and if she loved you, she would have left her boyfriend immediately."

A very simple deduction that threw me back onto my lonely path.

Werther had at least one trusty friend, Wilhelm, and he could talk about his troubles with him. I didn't even have that.

I suppose I stopped socializing out of fear of

being let down again. As an adolescent I got fed up with doing what other people wanted, only to be left high and dry when I needed them. Then again, it's not easy to find people with whom you can have a vaguely interesting conversation.

I turned on the radio and fiddled with the dial until I found a music program. They were broadcasting a jam session from Tokyo. The audience started to applaud just as I finished flipping my omelet.

Interpreting the clapping as an ovation for the cook, I bowed a couple of times to show my appreciation and then went back to my dinner.

I was in bed by eleven with the lights off, although I was still listening to the broadcast. Four great masters of jazz played with a fifth who was celebrating the fiftieth anniversary of his first concert on that stage.

Staring at the dark ceiling and listening to the competing virtuosi, I suddenly remembered the dead Japanese man.

I started to feel anxious. *Maybe he fell ill during the night, but there was nobody around to help him. That must be why they say that married men live longer than bachelors. For example, if I had a heart attack right now . . .*

A strange sensation in my chest left me breathless. Fumbling for the phone, I felt cold drops of sweat running down my forehead. I knocked the handset onto the floor. Trembling all over, I managed to turn on my bedside light. Then I saw them.

Two round green eyes, staring at me.

The cat.

It must have hidden somewhere in my apartment, but now it was sitting on my chest, gazing at me as if seeking answers.

"You bastard!" I shouted, leaping out of bed as the cat fled into the living room. "I nearly had a heart attack!"

The situation demanded that I resort to extreme measures, so I grabbed the broom from the kitchen and sprang into the living room like a wild beast, determined to drive out the intruder.

No cat.

I leaned the broom against the wall and checked every corner without success. I did the same in the bedroom. The cat wasn't hiding among the blankets or under the bed or in the slightly open closet.

My second search of the living room was as fruitless as the first, and I scoured the whole apartment with the same result. The cat was clearly a genius when it came to hiding and wasn't going to make my life easy.

I was overwhelmed by a sense of deep weariness. A shooting pain in my back warned me to stop stooping over and forced me back into bed.

"I've lost the battle but not the war," I

proclaimed aloud. "Tomorrow I'm going to turn the place upside down. I'll get you in the end. Just you wait and see."

I got into bed and fell asleep almost at once. I didn't even turn off the radio. The jam session had finished.

First Victories

I woke up with a strange vibrating feeling in my breastbone. I didn't need to open my eyes to know that this wasn't a warning sign of a heart attack.

To my great surprise I saw that the cat was curled up, placidly asleep on my chest.

"You're a stubborn animal," I said, wondering if I should throttle it there and then.

Almost out of curiosity, I stroked its short, soft fur. The cat revved up its purring and opened its sleepy eyes. Then it began to stretch, raising its back and shifting its paws, and ended up sitting on my belly. It was still purring and seemed to be smiling.

Can a cat smile?

After breakfast, I decided that the intruder could stay until the animal shelter opened. I found the number in the phone book but, when I called, a tinny voice informed me that they were closed until January 7th.

Then I remembered that I'd seen a pets section in the *Pennysaver*.

It could be an option in case the shelter won't take it. I rummaged around in my storage room, trying to find an old copy of the paper, which I'd occasionally consulted when I wanted to buy second-hand furniture.

I phoned the number, and an affected voice promptly answered. I mentioned the section in which the ad would appear and dictated: "Almost new cat. Free of charge. Excellent condition. Phone afternoons."

I thought a touch of humor might help to find a home for the animal. It seemed that the operator didn't agree.

"Is that all?" he asked after jotting down my phone number.

"I think so."

"I can't take this ad as it is. What about its shots?"

"What?" I didn't know what he was talking about.

"We only take ads for vaccinated animals. The paper can't be held responsible in case of infection. You need to make it clear it's had its shots."

I was about to confess that I didn't know whether the cat was vaccinated or not, but bit my tongue.

"It's been vaccinated," I lied. "Put that at the end of the ad."

"OK."

According to the operator, I was in luck. They were closed that day, but they'd publish my ad on January 8th. I decided I would postpone my trip to the animal shelter for another week after that date. I needed time to see if some charitable soul would take the cat. And anyway, there was still the issue of its vaccinations. Anyone who came would want to see the certificates.

The cat was now comfortably installed on the couch, observing me as I pondered all these questions. Without changing its elegant pose, it studied my movements around the living room, restlessly flicking its tail.

Since I tend to deal with bothersome chores as quickly as possible, I picked up the phone book again, this time to find a vet. There were several clinics, and one was quite close to my place, so I called to book an appointment.

A brusque female voice answered.

"Your reason for the visit?"

"It's for a cat. It needs a vaccination certificate."

"Name?"

"Samuel de Juan."

"And the cat?"

This took me unawares. *Must all animals have a name?* I was standing next to a bookshelf full of novels, and my eyes lit on *The Sailor Who Fell from Grace with the Sea.*

"Mishima," I said.

The cat gave a loud meow, as if it was happy to be named after a Japanese writer who committed suicide by hara-kiri.

"What did you say?"

I spelled out the name, realizing that I was now faced with a logistical problem. How was I going to take the cat to the vet? It had proved to be very good at disappearing, and I had no wish to chase it around the streets. I explained my problem to the woman on the other end of the phone.

"You'll need a transporter box."

"A . . . transporter box? What is that?"

Mishima seemed to be relishing the situation. The rate of tail flicks per minute had risen considerably.

The woman informed me that it was an authorized container for carrying animals. She suggested I should come to the veterinary center to buy one and then bring the cat back in it.

"That's too much running around," I said, irritated. "I can't waste the whole day on a cat. Is there any other way?"

"A home visit—but that's a lot more expensive."

"That's fine. I want to get this over and done with as soon as possible."

"I'll have to come myself," was her sharp reply. "I'm on call now. Would lunchtime suit you?"

I said it would and took the opportunity to order all the cat paraphernalia I needed: bowl, food, litter, tray—and the transporter box too.

The doorbell rang at two thirty, and I knew it must be the vet because I never have visitors. When I opened the door, I was pleasantly surprised. The vet was an attractive woman of about thirty, short hair brushed back from her face, glasses. Her serious yet relaxed expression suggested that she was a no-nonsense kind of lady.

She's just the sort of person I'd like to have as a friend.

I could picture myself having afternoon tea with her—hot chocolate and ladyfingers—in one of the old establishments in Carrer Petritxol.

"Well, shall we begin?" she said in a brisk tone, shattering my daydream. "I'm very busy today."

"Of course."

After taking the two bags she was carrying, I asked her to come into the living room, where Mishima had spent the whole morning. When we walked in, the couch was empty.

"Where's the cat then?" she asked as she placed her small case on the table and opened it.

I rushed into the bedroom to see if Mishima was back on the bed. He wasn't there. I looked in the kitchen, where I had placed his saucer of milk. No luck. When I returned to the living room, the vet was already closing her case and getting ready to leave.

"Could you wait just a moment, please?" I said. "I'm sure the cat will turn up."

"I doubt it. Cats always hide when they're going to be vaccinated. Didn't you know that? You should have locked it up so you'd know where to find it."

"I must admit I know nothing about cats. Would you like a cup of coffee? I have a few questions I wanted to ask."

"I'm sorry. I've got another appointment at three," she said. "I came to look after the cat, not you."

I was hurt by her response. I grabbed the bill from her hand and paid the whole amount—including the fee for a home visit—plus a generous tip, because I had no change.

"When you find it," she said, as I ushered her toward the door, "put it in the cat carrier and bring it to the clinic. There's no need to make an appointment."

I nodded. Before we reached the front door, the vet pointed at a dollop of curdled white purée next to the rug. I hadn't noticed it before.

"Don't give your cat any more milk. It doesn't agree with them and makes them vomit."

I thanked her and closed the door.

Less than two minutes later Mishima reappeared and greeted me with a melodious meow, as if nothing had happened. His hiding place remained a secret.

"Great work," I said. "You naughty little beast."

The Old Editor

Third day of the new year. I woke up with aching bones, feeling feverish. The flu had obviously overcome my last defenses.

Mishima jumped off the bed and we went to have breakfast, each from his own bowl like two bachelor roommates. This exceptional situation was going to end no later than January 15th.

When I stood up from the table, I felt dizzy. I opened my medicine drawer, and all I could find was a bottle of painkillers—but it was empty.

I'll have to go down to the pharmacy before it gets worse.

A man who lives alone must be twice as organized as one who has a partner, because at the end of the day he has only his own resources to rely on.

Without bothering to take off my pajamas, I threw on the first clothes I could find, thinking I'd go out and be back in a moment.

Then, something unexpected happened. I was on the landing, about to lock the door, when Mishima shot out and raced upstairs.

"Damn cat!" I yelled, my voice echoing through the staircase.

It was clear that this cat had not come into

my life to make things easier. My forehead was burning now. I went inside to get the cat carrier. I'd catch the cat and lock it up inside—until January 15th if necessary.

Fortunately, there is only one more floor above mine. I was hoping to corner the cat and take it back home. But I was beginning to realize that a cat never does what one expects it to do.

Mishima was sitting on the doormat of the apartment above mine, calmly and patiently scratching at the door, just as he had done at my place three days before.

All my problems were over! The cat belonged to the old man on the top floor. He was a surly-looking individual, as bald as an egg, and it was hard to guess his age, although the mesh of deep wrinkles that lined his forehead and neck made me think he was on the wrong side of seventy. He was already living there when I moved into my place six years before, but I'd rarely seen him, except for the odd encounter on the stairway.

I rang the bell, and the door unlocked with a loud buzz. I pushed it open, and the cat marched inside right away. So my guess was right.

I entered the apartment without really knowing why. After all, now that the cat had been returned to its master, everything was back to normal.

A sweetish smell floated in the air, like musk in a spice burner.

"Hello," I called, closing the door behind me. I

didn't feel like chasing the cat downstairs if it escaped again.

Nobody answered.

I advanced down the corridor, which was similar to mine. Before I reached the living room, I stopped to look at a painting that had caught my attention. It was a reproduction of *Wanderer Overlooking the Sea of Fog* by the German Romantic painter Caspar David Friedrich.

In my student years I'd been fascinated by his work. In one of his bleakest paintings, *The Sea of Ice*, one can make out the shape of a wrecked ship, barely visible beneath a pyramid formed by the piled-up shards of a broken ice sheet.

The *Wanderer* shows a gentleman standing all alone on a high cliff, hair tousled by the wind as he contemplates the turbulent ocean of mist spreading out below him. It could very well have been a picture of Werther before his decision to put an end to it all.

I'd seen this painting many times. I think I even got to see the original in a gallery in Hamburg. Anyway, the *Wanderer* suddenly acquired a new meaning for me. I realized that it was an allegory of my life. I was this man who'd climbed a mountain without understanding what was happening down below in the world.

"Are you coming in or not?" a voice called from the living room.

"Sorry, are you speaking to me?"

"Who else?" There was a burst of laughter.

I went into the living room to sort out the matter of the cat and leave. The old man was sitting at a modern desk in the middle of the room. Without sparing a glance at me, he continued to type away at his laptop. At his side lay a popular-science book, *A Short History of Nearly Everything*. That was where I'd read about the 650,000 hours.

Before he looked up at me, I had time to notice a smaller table next to him, on top of which was a miniature train set, the kind that children of my generation used to have. The cat had made itself comfortable on the thick rug under the table.

"What is it, then?" The old man spoke in a surprisingly gentle tone.

"I was chasing a cat. I suppose it's yours?"

"You're wrong."

Mishima was licking his paw and cleaning his face with it. It was clear that this wasn't the first time he had been under that table.

"Who does it belong to, then?"

"The cat belongs to himself, just like you and me."

The old man went back to his typing, leaving me to stare at the toy railway and the cover of the book with its floating globe of the world.

"I used to have that book, but I ended up giving it away," I remarked, rather surprised at myself for divulging this information to a stranger.

"Why?" He still didn't look up from the screen. "It's a magnificent book."

"Science depresses me. It's a terrible thing to be a bunch of atoms waiting to be disassembled. I find no consolation in knowing that they'll recombine to form a pile of manure or, if I'm lucky, a patch of mushrooms."

"Obviously you haven't understood a thing," he said, turning off the laptop and closing the lid. "Science is a shortcut to God. In fact, if you look at the biographies of the greatest scientists, you'll find that they were all mystics."

"That may be true, but it's got nothing to do with what I was saying. What bothers me is that 650,000 hours after my birth, my atoms and molecules are going to form things without my permission."

"Atoms and molecules are nothing."

"Well, I thought they were everything," I countered. "Except for the void, of course, which is everywhere in the universe—even on a molecular level."

"Forget about the void. Right now, the biggest void I can see is in your head."

He gazed at me intently, as if trying to gauge my reaction. I remained silent. The man was beginning to fascinate me.

He continued. "Atoms are like letters. The same ones that make up the *Songs of Kabir* or the Canticles from the Bible are also used for articles in gossip magazines and ads for hair lotions. Do you see what I'm getting at?"

"No."

"I'll give you another example, then. The same blocks of stone can be used by Gaudí to build the Sagrada Familia or by someone else to put up the walls of Auschwitz. What's important is not the building material but the use that's made of it. Do you follow me now?"

"I think so."

"So when we talk about building blocks, letters, or atoms, what matters is who arranges them and what use is made of them. In other words, what we are isn't important. What we do with what we are is important. Hours are worthless unless you know what to do with them."

I didn't know what to say to that. I was shocked. I didn't expect this kind of conversation with the old man in the upstairs apartment. The silence began to feel uncomfortable, so I asked: "Are you a scientist?"

"Cold, cold!"

"Philosopher?"

"Freezing cold. I'm a simple editor who likes poking around at the fringes of knowledge."

"Editor . . . so do you write articles too?"

"If I wrote articles, I'd have said I'm a journalist. I said 'editor.' My job is to fiddle with texts from here and there and cobble together the books publishers ask for."

"Put like that, it sounds very easy." I sat on his couch without asking permission.

"It is if you know the sources—by which I mean if you know where to look. When they ask me for an anthology of love poems, I know which ones the readers like and where to find them. If they want a manual of natural remedies, I also know which works I need to consult. I suppose I'm a sort of book cobbler."

I didn't know such a job existed. I'd always imagined that all books were written by authors who were experts in the field.

"May I ask what you are 'cobbling together' now?" I asked.

He gave me a wry smile. "This one's a difficult job because, besides having to scour through many books, I have to collect interviews. Maybe you'd like to contribute to it?"

"What's it about?"

"The book's called *Take a Break*. It's a collection of inspirational stories told by people who've had a magical experience, something like a satori. You know, when time seems to stop."

"I don't think I can help," I said. "I don't remember having any experience like that. My life isn't very exciting, you know. Unless it's satori I experience when I'm flipping an omelet."

"What a shame," he said. "Well, maybe you'll help me in another way. Since you've come into my house, cat and all, and it seems that you're

44

having trouble leaving, perhaps you can do me a favor."

"Of course."

The old man swiveled his chair around to face the train set. "By the way," he said, as he removed a section of the tracks, "my name's Titus. It's a slightly unusual name, so I always use a pseudonym."

I introduced myself, watching in puzzlement as the old man extracted one of the curved pieces of the tracks and handed it to me with a smile.

"For some reason, this has gotten warped and it keeps derailing the trains."

"What would you like me to do?" I asked, still perplexed.

"My legs are a bit weak these days. The cold weather has brought on an attack of rheumatism. Anyway, the model-train shop is in the center of town. It's not far for a young fellow like yourself."

I shouldn't have agreed to help him. With my temperature rising by the minute, the last thing I wanted to do was to traipse across the city looking for a piece of toy train track.

"Aren't you rather too old for toy trains?" I said.

He struggled to his feet and gave me a gentle pat on the back.

"I find it relaxing, when I'm thinking, to watch the trains go around. Having a point on which you can focus your attention is always good for meditation."

"By the way," I said, pocketing the piece of track, "just out of curiosity—what's the cat's real name?"

The cat had not moved from under the table, where it had curled up and gone to sleep.

"How would I know? Ask him. I told you, he's not my cat. But I'll look after him while you go to the shop."

Gabriela

By the time I went out onto the street, my head was burning. After stopping briefly by the pharmacy, I looked for a taxi, but in vain. They were all full, probably because people were going into the city center to do some last-minute shopping.

They're maxing out their credit cards, and I'm going to get seriously ill because of a piece of toy train track.

Angry with the old man, I staggered to Carrer Balmes, where I could get the 16 or 17 bus to the shop in Carrer Pelai. During the twenty minutes I waited at the stop, nothing but blasts of a murderous wind came down the street. Then I saw a notice saying that the drivers were on strike.

Cursing my bad luck, I began to stride down Carrer Balmes. If I could keep up this pace I'd be there in about twenty minutes. There were times when I felt so weak I nearly gave up, but somehow I managed to make it.

I got there at one o'clock. A languid shop assistant in a blue dust coat examined the piece of track and said, "I don't know if I have any left. This model has been discontinued."

He disappeared into the storeroom at the back,

which I imagined was full of boxes containing miniature railway lines of every possible shape and gauge.

"You're in luck," the assistant informed me on his return, holding out a segment identical to the one I'd shown him. "It's the last one we have in this series. If you'd asked for a straight piece, you'd have left empty-handed."

I made no comment and proceeded to pay. It seemed a ridiculously small amount for such an arduous journey. The shop assistant handed me my purchase, neatly wrapped in brown paper, and I left the shop.

When the light turned green, I crossed the street, thinking about the fastest way to get home. I was right in the middle when the light changed to amber. It was then that I saw her.

The woman was more or less my age, tall and slim, with long, wavy black hair. Her slightly almond-shaped eyes and the freckles scattered on her cheeks confirmed that it was her. I'd caught only a quick glimpse of her when we were facing each other. From her bemused look, I knew she'd recognized me too.

Time suddenly seemed to stop, like a satori in the old man's book. Then the past shot forward with astounding clarity.

I was transported to a Saturday afternoon thirty years ago that I thought I had forgotten. I'd gone with my sister to a mansion on La Rambla, just as we did every weekend. It had a sweeping marble staircase and lots of places to hide. We went there because one of her school friends lived next door. The kids in the neighborhood regularly met there to play whatever games they came up with. That day it was the old classic, hide-and-seek.

I went to hide under some stairs, but someone had beaten me to it, a little girl aged six, like me, with curly black hair and glowing eyes.

"Do you know what a butterfly kiss is?" she whispered.

"No." I was scared. "What's that?"

She opened and shut her eyes a couple of times, her eyelashes brushing my cheek.

I never completely forgot that little girl, even though I never saw her again. Until now. Yes, it was her, no doubt about that, and she'd just crossed the street after pausing for an instant when we met midway.

Strange as it may seem, I had the feeling that, in essence, she hadn't changed.

In that fraction of a second I knew I'd always loved Gabriela. I still remembered her name. I realized in a flash that she was the love of my life, that I could never love anyone else as I'd loved that little girl who gave me a butterfly kiss under the stairs. There was no explanation. I simply knew it.

The satori was broken as the light turned red

and we hurried across the street in opposite directions. When I got to the other side, I turned around and saw she'd done the same, giving me a faint smile before continuing on her way.

I wished I could stop her, have coffee with her, and ask about her life, but traffic had taken over the street again, wiping out all traces of a path back to the past.

I must have raised my arm, because a taxi driver, thinking I had signaled to him, stopped just in front of me. I mechanically got in and mumbled my address. Slumped in the backseat, I could feel my heart pounding in a strange way and a tight sensation in my stomach that I had not experienced since adolescence.

As we weaved our way through the traffic, I had a moment of lucidity. The revelation had come to me only seconds after the reappearance—and loss—of Gabriela.

It was so obvious that anyone else might think that carrying on about it was pointless. But I welcomed it as a revelation. Somehow it dawned on me that Gabriela, my childhood love, had come back to me because I'd filled a saucer with milk. There was no apparent link between the two things, but they were connected at a deeper level.

After I had poured milk into his saucer, the cat had hidden away in my apartment. Then he had led me to the old man, the old man to the model-train shop—and to Gabriela.

The piece of train track in my pocket now acquired a transcendental meaning. That aluminum curve had led me off my path into the arms of a ghost from my past.

Now I knew that our future depends on such tiny acts as feeding a cat or buying a section of model-train track.

But what did all this mean? Did I have to search for Gabriela? Should I go back and pick up my life where I'd left it thirty years earlier? Where did the links of this chain lead?

Love in lowercase, that's the secret. I felt as if the words didn't come from me but from a sunbeam shining through the taxi window, lighting up a galaxy of dust motes.

One thing was clear: without that saucer of milk, I wouldn't have run into Gabriela. That's where it all began.

II

The Dark Side
of the Moon

Epiphany

The flu kept me in bed, faint and dizzy, for three whole days that dragged by like a long, tedious nightmare. Mishima hardly moved from my side the whole time. As if he knew the worst was over, he moved closer, purring and nuzzling my cheek with his head, saying something along the lines of: "Get your act together. It's time you got up. You have things to do. I need food and water, and you have to clean my litter box."

I glanced at the alarm clock, mainly to find out what day it was, as I'd lost all sense of time: January 6th, 10:44 a.m.

So, Epiphany today. I tested the cold floor with my foot. I still felt weak, but the fever had gone and a gnawing hunger told me I was back on the road to normal existence. Unfortunately, this meant having lunch at my sister's, although the flu would give me a good excuse for not going.

A quick inspection of my apartment revealed that during my illness I'd been moving around like a restless ghost. I didn't remember filling Mishima's bowl, but the cat food scattered on the floor confirmed that at least I'd tried to feed him.

After filling up his water bowl, I looked at the dining room. A note lay on the table with something scribbled in big letters. It was my own writing: I'd jotted down a description of my encounter with Gabriela at the traffic light. *So it wasn't a dream.* A sweet sensation of euphoria swept through my body.

I turned on the radio and set about cleaning the kitchen counter, which was covered with spilled broth and grains of rice, evidence of my attempts to feed myself during my illness. The notes of Verdi's *Requiem* filled the air. I turned the radio off and checked the morning sky from the kitchen window. Just then, a sparrow flew by with something in its beak.

I'll have lunch with my sister. I don't know why I decided that. Yet, I did have a reason—a plan even—but I wasn't aware of it at the time, as if there was a secret operations center inside me that only reported when everything was ready to go.

What we call intuition is perhaps only the tip of the iceberg, something that has been taking shape at a deeper level. This thought was disturbing, to say the least, because it means that someone— which is to say one's self, working in the shadows—knows about one's actions in advance and decides beforehand what path one has to take.

As I walked past the phone, I could see that the answering machine wasn't flashing. I'd been cut off from the world for three days. It could have been three years and nobody would have known—just like the man in Tokyo.

Mishima started to weave himself around my legs, trying to get my attention.

"Yes, I know you're here," I told him. "And we have Titus upstairs. We're three wise men, but we don't know whom to give our gifts to."

Then it occurred to me that it wouldn't be a bad idea to go upstairs and visit Titus before going out for lunch. I looked at the bit of paper on the table. He'd certainly be happy that I could offer him a golden moment for his collection.

The Cosmic Slot Machine

I gave Titus the piece of paper. He held it in his hand as if he didn't know what to do with it and listened attentively to my story. When I finished, he remained wrapped in thought for a few moments.

As I waited for his response, I noticed the old man's sallow complexion. He didn't look good at all. Shrunken inside his gray dressing gown, he seemed like a wounded animal awaiting the coup de grâce. I was about to ask him about his health when he decided to answer.

"I'll include your satori in the book."

"Don't you think it's a little silly?"

"Not in the least."

"What I mean to say is that now I've seen her, I can't just hang around twiddling my thumbs as if nothing happened. I know it's ridiculous, but I think I have to do something."

"So do it."

"The problem is that I don't know anything about her other than her first name. And what if I found her? What could I tell her so that she wouldn't think I'm a weirdo? I need a good excuse."

"You've got far too many excuses. Stop thinking about that and act!"

"Do you think I should go looking for her? Is that the meaning of what happened?"

"Absolutely. That's the mission you've been assigned."

"But who assigned it to me? Chance?"

"Or the shadow of God—or whatever you like to call it."

"I find it hard to believe that this is mere chance. I can't put it into words but, when our paths crossed, I knew that if she was there right then, it was for a reason. There was nothing fortuitous about it."

Titus drummed his fingers on top of his desk. "We refuse to accept chance if it crops up in our everyday lives, because it seems too whimsical. But we accept it in the universe and in the formation of life, which depends on an infinitely more whimsical conjunction of elements."

"What do you mean?"

"The probability of the emergence of life is about the same as hitting the jackpot on a slot machine with hundreds of reels. We're here because once upon a time the only combination that could work came up. Don't you think that's amazing? And who dropped in the coin to make the reels spin? That's the big mystery. The Big Bang is totally irrelevant because the main thing is not what happened, but who or what clicked a lighter to light the wick."

"Does that mean there's an invisible hand behind everything that happens to us?"

"That would be a gross oversimplification." Titus was smiling for the first time. "I believe it was Jung who said that all beings are joined by invisible threads. You pull one, and the whole set moves. This is why every small act affects everything and everyone. You don't need a God for that."

"But knowing this doesn't help me to understand why Gabriela was there—and still less what I'm supposed to do now."

"Remember the cosmic slot machine. The fact that we're here is already a mystery. A great mystery. That's all there is to it."

The Opposite Is Best

My conversation with an out-of-sorts Titus had hardly clarified matters. In some way he was urging me to do something, but he didn't specify what or how. Perhaps the best thing would be to stop wasting time with romantic fantasies and forget about the whole thing once and for all.

Before saying good-bye, I told him how reluctant I was to go to my sister's.

"Well, I can offer you a magic formula for that," he said.

When I asked what it was, he said, "The opposite is best. Whenever you're angry with someone, apply this maxim. It means doing the exact opposite of what your body's telling you to do. Believe me, it works miracles."

While waiting in line at the bakery to buy the Epiphany cake, the *tortell de Reis*, I decided I'd try to follow Titus's advice.

Rita and Andreu—my sister and her husband—form a duo that is as perfect as it is destructive. He has taken on the role of chief mourner and complains nonstop, while her job is to point at the guilty parties.

In the fifteen years they've been together, I don't remember ever seeing a happy moment in that house. I always put it down to their not having had children as they'd wished. Now Rita is well over forty, and I suppose she's come to terms with the fact that nothing's going to change. Including her disagreeable character.

As I went up in the elevator to their apartment in Avinguda Diagonal, a cold sweat broke out on the nape of my neck. It always happens when I visit them. Knowing I was going to be there for a couple of hours made me feel queasy even before arriving. It's a psychosomatic thing.

The opposite is best. I repeated this mantra as I rang the bell.

Andreu opened the door, and the mere sight of his wounded-bull expression made me regret that I hadn't prolonged my flu for one more day and stayed home.

"How are you?"

I knew he didn't care how I was, but I applied Titus's maxim and said: "I've been ill for the past three days. But you look great."

"Really?" He was taken aback.

"I can't believe you had a hernia operation only two months ago. You look ten years younger, as if you've been to a spa."

I went into the dining room, leaving a deflated Andreu at the door. *This could be fun.*

"What did you say? Are you drunk?" were my sister's words of welcome. "Or are you messing with him as usual?"

I hugged my sister and planted a kiss on her forehead.

"So good to see you," I said. "Sorry I didn't bring gifts this year."

"Since when do we exchange gifts?" Rita said, showing me into the living room.

"Since today." I laughed. "I was thinking . . . perhaps we could go out to a seafood restaurant one Sunday? My treat."

My sister's face relaxed, giving way to a cautious smile.

"That's very nice of you, but Andreu's on a diet and I turned vegetarian last month."

"Good for you," I said, humoring her. "Meat's full of hormones and all sorts of nasties."

"Well, at least you're not arguing with me for once," she said, and went into the kitchen to see to the food.

I sat down next to Andreu, who, with a glass of water in his hand, was spellbound by the news on TV. He kept casting sideways glances at me as if afraid that I really was drunk and would end up doing something silly.

"What a state the world's in! Terrible," he ventured. "Where will we all end up?"

"Something's got to be done—and soon."

I caught him unawares.

"You think something can be done about it?" he said.

"Of course. For a start, they should fire the

news editor and put in another one who gives us more pleasant news."

Rita came in with a dish of vegetarian lasagna and put it on the table. "What's going on with you? From the moment you arrived, you've been talking nonsense."

Normally we would have sat down at the table and eaten in silence, watching the news. Titus's maxim prompted me to try to do the opposite. I praised every dish my sister served, took an interest in what was going on in their lives, and told them a couple of anecdotes to liven up the atmosphere.

"A cat got into my apartment," I informed them between mouthfuls. "At first I thought it belonged to Titus, but it looks like it doesn't have an owner."

"Who's Titus?" Andreu asked, turning off the television with the remote control.

"I think it's great that you've got a cat," Rita said, before I could answer. "It'll give you good vibes. They absorb negative energy, you know."

The old Samuel would have said, "That's why I was thinking of giving it to you," but instead I took the conversation into uncharted territory, reminding her of what we used to do on Saturday afternoons thirty years earlier. I also asked if she'd heard any news of Gabriela.

"Who is she? I don't remember that name," she

said. "There are lots of kids from the Gothic Quarter. We only knew a few of them."

"She hid under the stairs with me. I think you were the one who found us."

"How can I remember that? Anyway, if she was under the stairs, she must have been a devil."

"I thought you didn't believe in that stuff."

"Why do you think people keep away from places like that? I think it's written in the Bible: the devil hides there."

The conversation then moved on to aromatherapy, a discipline my sister had recently taken up. I realized it was time to go. I downed my coffee and put an end to my visit.

"Get some sleep," Rita said with a sardonic expression as she waved good-bye. "I think the flu's gotten to your brain."

How to Become Enlightened in One Weekend

That afternoon, my Epiphany gift to myself was correcting the laggards' essays. Some couldn't even spell Werther's name. I gave some of them a pass out of compassion. Others were given a reprieve so that I wouldn't have to read their stuff again in September. I'd become pragmatic.

I bundled up the essays in my folder ready for the next morning. My first class was with that group.

The light was fading. I switched on my reading lamp so that I could read a few more entries in Rheingold's dictionary before dinner. I was struck by his definition of a German word that is no longer used much these days.

Weltschmerz: literally, "world-weariness."

The word seemed to have been created for Goethe's hero. At the end of his entry, Rheingold points out that *Weltschmerz* sufferers are often the sons or (less frequently) daughters of rich parents who don't have to worry about their next meal or having a roof over their heads and are therefore free to indulge in a feeling of existential malaise.

This definition made me think of my sister.

Although she didn't have a Romantic bone in her body, Rita had made it very clear as an adolescent that the world was piling its pain upon her. And how!

Maybe it's because our mother died when we were very young, and we were left in the care of a man who neglected us because of his other priorities. Rita had inherited my mother's apartment, where she now lives with her husband, and I got some shares that I never touched, plus a feeling of bitterness that still lingers on.

Rita and I were quite close until she turned twenty. Even though she had become despotic and nasty by then, as an adolescent she still thought she could change. I called her the "course kid," because she was always trying something new: Tai Chi, Reiki, Biodanza, and so on.

She was trying to feel good about herself, a sheer egotistical impulse that didn't bear any fruit. Then again, I found her amusing. She always had something new to talk about, and I listened with curiosity, even though I didn't think any of that stuff could make a person happy.

I remember that one weekend—I was a university student then—I agreed to go along with her to a course of what in those days was called "transcendental meditation." The guru was a tanned fiftysomething. He had rented a farmhouse in the Empordà region, where—the leaflet informed us—we would share the miraculous experience of enlightenment after just one weekend.

I found myself in an attic with about twenty other young people who were avid to learn what existence was all about.

After breakfast on the Saturday morning, the guru summoned us to the garden for a chat. He began by dismissing the "false gurus"—that is to say, his competitors—and assured us that enlightenment was within the reach of all those who dared open their eyes.

"And you're already enlightened," he told us. "But the thing is, you don't know it yet."

Everything was pretty normal until then. After that, we went into a hall, where each one was given a thick mat and a hard pillow. The guru told us everything about the lotus position and the half-lotus position, warning us that it might take us some time to master them. For the time being, he would let us sit with our backs straight and eyes half closed.

"Every second in which you manage to keep your mind clear," he proclaimed in a deep voice, "is a crack in your armor through which tenderness and clarity may enter."

The guru turned out to be full of love, especially for the women with the best bodies. He kept helping them to correct their posture. He was particularly concerned that, when they breathed in, they had to lift their chest, and he checked this from behind with his hands on their breasts. The women weren't allowed to wear a bra during meditation because he said it "restricted the breath of life." I think I must have been very skilled at breathing and meditating as he never had to help me.

That Saturday night there was a great commotion when he chose a young girl for Tantric Initiation. He'd lavished attention on her during the meditation exercise, and now she was refusing the privilege, saying she wasn't ready. The guru was furious and ridiculed her in front of the group. "Until you get rid of your petit bourgeois hang-ups, there is no hope of liberation for you."

What was clear to me was that the guru was very far from penetrating the deep folds of reality. One could generously say that the light of his enlightenment was forty watts at most.

Franz and Milena

After a boring essay-writing class, I gave a lesson on contemporary literature to my fourth-year students. There were eight of them, quite a nice group, and they were fluent in German, even though it was a struggle to get them to read a whole book.

Since this was an introductory course, we spent two weeks on each author. I gave a short presentation with some biographical information and a few details about the works we were studying. I gave the students a subject to prepare and asked them to talk about it in class.

This is the way they teach humanities in Germany. In Spain, however, it's hard to get students to take any initiative. Most of them prefer the traditional method, in which the lecturer dictates the same notes year after year and the students scribble away, never once raising their heads.

That day, the paper was on Franz Kafka. Many students feel intimidated by him because of the common prejudice that his books are difficult, but I argued that nothing could be further from the truth. In order to demonstrate this, I wrote on the blackboard the first sentences from two of his key works, *The Metamorphosis* and *The Trial*.

One morning, as Gregor Samsa woke from a fitful, dream-filled sleep, he found that he had changed into a monstrous insect.

Someone must have been slandering Josef K., because one morning, without having done anything wrong, he was arrested.

Before giving my students their assignment, I talked briefly about Kafka's life, skipping the obvious facts, such as his problems with his father. Instead, I focused on some of the more insignificant details—for example, the fact that he had an uncle in Madrid who got to be director-general of a railway company. I also told them that Kafka used to sleep every afternoon for four and a half hours, and that at the end of his life he dreamed of opening a restaurant in Tel Aviv and working there as a waiter.

I guess this is gossip culture infiltrating the classroom, but if you want to interest students you have to put yourself on their level.

I devoted the last twenty minutes of my lesson to Kafka's correspondence. Apart from his unfinished novels, he sent the women who loved him hundreds of wonderful letters. Probably the best among them were those he wrote to Milena Jesenská, who had translated some of his works into Czech.

Unlike Kafka, she wasn't Jewish, but after the

German army occupied Czechoslovakia she was deported and imprisoned in the Ravensbrück concentration camp, where she died in 1944. One could almost say that Franz Kafka was lucky to have died of tuberculosis twenty years earlier.

Their love was doomed because, among other things, she was married. However, this didn't prevent them from meeting a couple of times or stop Kafka from writing her the following words:

> Dear Frau Milena, the day is so short, what with the time spent with you and a few trivial things it is almost over and done with. There's hardly any time left to write to the real Milena, since the even more real one was here the whole day, in the room, on the balcony, in the clouds.

Lunatic

Kafka's love letters must have put me in a romantic mood, because when I left the class I decided to return to the crime scene.

It was 1:00 p.m., the same time as when we had met. The intersection where it happened was only a few minutes' walk from the university. This time I felt no emotion. The street looked like any other street, with its never-ending traffic of buses, cars, and motorbikes.

This street is much worse when Gabriela's not crossing it. I laughed at my own observation.

On the other side of the street there was a small bar with a terrace, at the beginning of Carrer Bergara. I thought it wouldn't be a bad idea to sit there for a while to see if the miracle might happen again. While I was heading for the only free table, I remembered the joke about the drunk man who, on his way home at night, looks for his keys next to a lamppost, not because he lost them there, but because there's more light. I was doing much the same, but only to prolong a dream.

Although it was sunny, I was surprised to see that two out of the three tables on the terrace were occupied in the middle of winter. An elderly couple was sitting at one of them—

73

Scandinavians, by the look of it. I guess a temperature of five degrees and icy gusts of wind must have been like summer for them. A bearded man of about forty in a gray overcoat, wide-brimmed black hat, and white scarf sat at the other table, holding a thick, spiral-bound manuscript.

I took my seat at the free table in the middle and asked for a vermouth. From there I had an excellent view of the intersection, although there was no guarantee I'd be able to catch Gabriela if she turned up.

What a coincidence, Gabriela!—I'd say—*The other day I was devastated I didn't have a chance to say hello.*

Me too. Isn't it a miracle that we've met up again after so many years?

It's chance that brought us back together again. But sometimes one has to help it along, like God.

Well, that doesn't matter. The most important thing is that we're together now, isn't it?

Yes, nothing will separate us now.

As I imagined this conversation and began to feel emotional, I noticed that the bearded man was openly staring at me. I tried to stare him down, but he didn't flinch. He seemed to be mesmerized by my presence.

I conceded defeat and looked down at the manuscript on his table. It was a thick book of more than three hundred pages with the following title, written in large letters:

THE DARK SIDE OF THE MOON

Must be a nutcase. I paid and stood up to leave my observation post. The man in the hat kept studying me, and even as I walked away I could feel his lunatic's gaze boring into my back.

Message in a Bottle

I had a sandwich on the run for lunch, as I didn't want to waste too much time: back home I had an ambitious domestic program that included two loads of laundry, vacuuming the living-roomrug, and cooking dinner for the whole week.

I was also keen to work on my Kafka notes. I wanted to be on the ball when my students started their oral presentations.

After three Metro stops I was in Gràcia, the only neighborhood in Barcelona where there is more space for pedestrians than for cars. When I passed the Verdi movie complex on my way home, I stopped to see what was showing. Then I bought a newspaper and a bottle of sparkling water.

I could now lock myself away until the following day.

When I walked through the door, I saw that my answering machine was flashing. There were two messages. I pressed the play button.

"Good morning," said a man's voice. "My name is Paco Liñán, and I'm calling about the cat. I'd like to see it before I make up my mind. My phone number is . . ."

I deleted the message. I'd decided that the cat

wasn't going anywhere. Mishima, strutting around the living room, his tail held high, seemed to know that already.

"Hello," said the second message. "This is the vet speaking. Since you haven't brought the cat in yet, I thought I'd phone you to remind you about the vaccinations. If you come, I won't charge you for the visit. *Ciao.*"

Good girl. We might yet have that hot chocolate and those ladyfingers together.

I took the vegetables out of the fridge and set them out on the kitchen counter. *Oops, we have a problem. One onion isn't enough.* Unfortunately, onion soup can't be short of onions.

I went upstairs to ask Titus if I could borrow one or two from him. I rang the bell, but this time the door didn't unlock with a buzz. I rang again. Silence.

I noticed a piece of paper sticking out from under the door. I immediately knew that the note was for me and that it wasn't good news.

Samuel, they've taken me to the Hospital Clinic. I need help urgently, and you're the only one who can provide it.

The Assignment

I had forgotten the hospital was such a labyrinthine and Kafkaesque place, full of dismal corridors and flickering neon lights. It took me half an hour to find the room that Titus shared with an old man with one foot in the grave.

When he saw me, he raised his hand with a smile. Unshaven, wearing green pajamas, Titus seemed to have aged ten years in one day. Seeing him in such a sorry state, with a drip in his arm, filled me with sadness. I tried to counter that feeling using Titus's own magic formula.

"So you've decided to take it easy at last. But this hotel doesn't have many stars."

"Stop it. I've had a bout of angina, but I'm not going to die just yet. I'm glad you've come."

A buxom nurse came in to attend to his roommate.

"You've got everything here," I joked. "Why did you say that I was the only one who could help you?"

"What I have to ask you has nothing to do with the hospital. It's a much more serious matter."

I sat down beside him.

"You know I make my living as an editor," he went on. "I can't slack off, even if I'm locked up here. They're saying I'll have to stay at least three weeks because there's a risk I may have another attack."

"Then you'll have to rest, no? If you need money, I can—"

"Thank you, but it's not about money," he interrupted. "It's about how I can get out of this mess. At my age, I can't fail to deliver. If I do, the publishers will give me the boot."

"I don't understand."

"You soon will. Two days ago I was sent a job by a pigheaded publisher. He's one of those people who won't tolerate delays. If he discovers that I'm ill, he'll find another editor, and I won't be asked again. I want him to keep sending me work when I get out of here."

"What have I got to do with all this? Do you want me to talk to him and tell him about your situation?"

"No! That's exactly what must be avoided. He must think that I'm working and that I'm going to meet the deadline. This is the first job in a batch of three, you see. If I don't deliver on time, I won't be asked again."

"I can't see how—"

"I'm asking you to take on the job for me, Samuel."

"What? You mean cobble together one of your inspirational books?"

"That's right. I'll supervise the job from here to make things easier. You can take my keys and use my office. You'll find the document in the computer."

If Titus hadn't just cheated death, I'd have gotten up and left. You can't really ask an academic who works with footnotes and critical bibliographies to do something like that.

"What's the title of the work?" I asked.

"A Short Course in Everyday Magic."

Marilyn's Last

On my way home I felt overwhelmed by what I'd let myself in for. As if I didn't have enough on my plate, what with preparing classes, correcting papers, and doing my housework! Now I also had to turn into an editor . . .

Before going into my apartment, I went upstairs to Titus's place. I opened the door and switched on the light in the hallway. At the end of it, the picture of the wanderer overlooking the sea of fog. I stopped to look at him.

All this to be even lonelier than I already was.

I'd read in the newspaper that 20.3 percent of the households in my country were occupied by only one person. I was part of that statistic, a "home man," the article said, a snail attached to a house in which there is only room for one.

OK, so now I was going to have two homes and two parallel lives. In my place I'd still be Samuel, lecturer in German Studies, and upstairs I'd spend a few hours every day being Titus. The worst of it was that I was taking on this split personality with disconcerting composure.

Whatever next!

I gazed at the old man's desk in the waning afternoon light. Everything was there: the laptop, the science book, the train set. Three books were scattered on the rug as if they'd fallen from Titus's hands when he had his bout of angina.

I knelt to pick them up. One was a collection of the most famous aphorisms by Siddhartha Gautama, the Buddha. The other two were biographies of Alan Watts and Thomas Merton.

I decided to take them home so I could start preparing for my new role. I wouldn't start working on the book until the following day, assuming I was able to do something about it.

At about eight o'clock that evening, I started to feel anxious. The recent events were a bit too much for me. The three books—my new bedtime reading—lay on my bedside table.

Suddenly I had a strong urge to get out of my apartment, even though I hadn't done any of the chores I intended to complete. They were showing one of my favorite films at the Verdi, *The Misfits*. I checked the newspaper to see if I had enough time to get there for the penultimate screening. I grabbed my coat and went out, with the feeling that I was running away from myself.

Before going into the auditorium, I hung around in the foyer reading a leaflet about the shooting of the film. What turned out to be Marilyn Monroe's last film—with a script by her husband, Arthur Miller—was a series of madcap events and disasters from start to finish.

The filming lasted 111 days. Apart from the blonde bombshell, the movie starred Clark Gable and Montgomery Clift. It soon became apparent that, like the characters they were enacting, none of the actors were in great shape.

Every day Marilyn arrived on the set hours late because she was taking so many prescription drugs that it was impossible to wake her up. It seems that she felt betrayed by her two lovers, John F. Kennedy and Yves Montand—not to mention Miller himself, who'd used her to make a comeback. When she eventually arrived on set, she wasn't much use because she'd forgotten her lines, or her expression was so blank that the director—John Huston—decided to call it a day.

At fifty-nine, Clark Gable wasn't in the best of health. This didn't stop him from downing two bottles of whiskey and smoking three packs of cigarettes every day. A true gentleman of the old school, he never got worked up over Marilyn's late arrivals. When she arrived, he merely said: "Let's get to work, honey."

As for Montgomery Clift, he was hooked on alcohol and drugs. His face had been disfigured in a car accident, and he was also trying to deal with his repressed homosexuality.

Faced with all this, John Huston lost interest in the film and spent his nights in a casino, going in at eleven and leaving at five in the morning. He racked up such huge gambling debts that—they say—he stopped shooting and sent Marilyn off to a hospital so he could sort out his own mess.

It was a miracle they managed to finish filming on November 5th, 1960. It must have been a grueling experience, because Clark Gable died of a heart attack a few days later. It was also Marilyn's last film. She took a lethal overdose not long afterward. To cap it all, *The Misfits* was a box-office disaster.

The leaflet ended with a eulogy for Marilyn written by the poet Ernesto Cardenal:

Lord / receive this young woman known around the world as Marilyn Monroe / [. . .] / who now comes before You without any makeup / without her press agent / without photographers and without autograph hounds / alone like an astronaut facing night in space.

Secret Garden

On my way to the intersection bar for the second time, the wild horses that Marilyn was trying to save in the film I had seen the previous day were still galloping through my head.

From a distance I could make out the figure of someone I didn't wish to see seated at one of the tables. The black hat and white scarf left me in no doubt: it was him.

I was tempted to turn around, walk away, and never go back there again, but the bearded man seemed so engrossed in his manuscript that I doubted he'd notice my presence. Indeed, when I sat down at the middle table, he didn't even look up. I could relax.

I asked for a vermouth and paid for it in advance as a precaution. That Thursday lunchtime, the hubbub of cars and pedestrians was even greater than usual, so I had to be on the lookout. I was so absorbed in studying the people moving about that it took me a while to realize that the bearded man had gone, leaving his manuscript on the table.

I thought I'd do my duty and give it to the waiter to keep for him. He must be a regular, so he'd get it back soon.

But now that I had the manuscript in my hands, I couldn't resist having a peek. I checked the title again—*The Dark Side of the Moon*—and started reading it.

Every light has its shadow. However simple they may appear to be, people conceal a world in which unthinkable things happen. If by chance we enter it, we are invaded by feelings of bewilderment and fear, as if we were trespassing in someone else's garden.

Suddenly we realize that we have been blind to something that has always been there. The next step is to extend the territory of doubt to adjoining spheres, whereupon the region of shadows can lead us into never-imagined realms. After all, the other side of a coin occupies the same area as the one you can see.

You might discover that you know nothing of the person living beside you, or that you have closed your eyes so as not to see. And you would then wish that this first revelation—which had ripped apart the sweet calm of your everyday existence—had never happened.

This is why sometimes it is better not to want to know everything.

After reading this, I sat there perplexed for a few moments. I didn't know what to make of it. Those first few lines didn't tell me what the book was about.

Intrigued, I decided to keep reading, but luckily I looked up. The bearded man was crossing at the traffic light, walking at a frantic pace. He wasn't angry with me. That was clear because he didn't even look at me: he was annoyed with himself because he'd committed the unforgiveable error of leaving his manuscript on the terrace.

Still, I left his book on the table and rushed away without looking back.

Draft Contents Page

I had a strange feeling when I got home. My encounter with the bearded man and his manuscript had set off alarm bells in my mind, as if reading what I shouldn't have read was going to have consequences—the butterfly effect unleashing a chain of small events with devastating results.

As I tried to find a radio station with decent music, I stopped at the sound of electric guitar from the 1970s, even though I usually prefer to listen to classical or jazz. The program was devoted to a Pink Floyd record on the occasion of one of its anniversaries.

"This is one of the most emblematic albums ever," said the radio announcer in a deep, relaxed voice. "It has sold more than twenty-five million copies since its first appearance in 1973. After rehearsing the songs live, the group cloistered itself away in the legendary Abbey Road Studios. The sound engineer was Alan Parsons, who recorded sixteen tracks using the new Dolby equipment to produce a true work of art. This is a recording full of stunning surprises—for example, the use of the voice of the studio's doorman, who didn't expect to be heard on the record. For all our listeners, we are delighted to present the remastered version of the classic *The Dark Side of the Moon*."

• • •

I shut myself away in Titus's office, trying to forget about the coincidence and recalling the old man's description of chance: "the shadow of God."

"No more shadows, please," I said out loud, while waiting for the laptop to boot up.

Mishima had followed me upstairs and was now asleep under the train-set table. A butane heater filled the room with soporific gas.

On the desktop I found a document called *A Short Course in Everyday Magic*. I clicked, and it opened fast: it contained very little text apart from the title.

Titus was using the name of Francis Amalfi for the anthology. This was just one of his many pseudonyms. Since I was supposed to be the one who had to write the book, this would now become my pen name and alter ego. Samuel de Juan, with a doctorate in Germanic Philology, could not be the author of a mass-market book.

I scrolled down the document and reached the list of contents. It was the only thing Titus had written; the rest of the book was blank. I read the chapter headings to see if I could come up with something that would fit with them.

Contents (draft)
0. Prologue: Welcome to Magic
1. The Treasures of Solitude

2. Everyday Caresses for the Soul
3. The Flowers of Chance
4. Heart in Hand
5.
6.
7.

Not much to go on. I felt exhausted at the mere idea of the amount of work in store for me. Titus had not even finished the contents page and expected me to turn this into a book!

Since I am a methodical person, I decided I had to complete the list of contents before starting to work on the book. I stared at the empty space to the right of number 5, hoping for a flash of brilliance. A sudden meow from Mishima shook me out of my stupor.

Thanks for the suggestion, Mishima. I started typing.

5. Feline Philosophy

Not a brilliant title, perhaps, but I found it amusing to devote a chapter to a cat—though I had no idea what the cat was going to say.

Encouraged by this, I moved on to number 6. Perhaps I could include a dictionary of sorts in the book. I could take some of the entries from *They Have a Word for It*, if I had nothing better to contribute. At least I had a title for the time being.

6. The Secret Language

Sounds good. Now I was really into it. Since one thing leads to another, I typed in the title of the last chapter almost without realizing it. The list of contents was complete.

7. Love in Lowercase

I regarded the last heading with pride. This was the only chapter I could imagine with a certain clarity. It would open with an introduction about the power of small actions. Then I would list things that can generate "love in lowercase."

I scrolled down to the bottom of the page and jotted down the first item.

No. 1: Give a cat some milk (even if the milk doesn't agree with it).

This reminded me that I had to go to the vet to get Mishima vaccinated. An attractive woman with a prickly character but a good heart was waiting for me there.

With the cat following behind, I stopped for a moment to look at the wanderer in the picture, which had turned into a sort of mirror.

"Let me know when the fog clears," I told him.

The Natural Canon
of Beauty

I was beginning to know a thing or two about feline behavior, so I kept my bedroom door closed all night to prevent Mishima from hiding somewhere in the house. He must have guessed what was awaiting him, because he was doing everything he could to get out.

When he worked out that scratching at the door was pointless, he started meowing and jumping onto the bed to wake me up, but I held my ground. He gave up in the end and was now curled up at my feet, fast asleep.

Before getting myself some breakfast, I locked him in the cat carrier. As I tried to calm him by stroking his head through the grille, his meow turned into a moan.

"That's life," I told him. "Don't take it personally."

Before us at the vet's clinic was a slobbering pit bull terrier that kept glowering at us in a threatening way. Its young skinhead owner didn't look friendly either. I could almost feel Mishima bristling inside the carrier. At least he'd be happy to be locked up inside it now.

The consulting-room door opened, and a lilac-haired old lady came out with a poodle in her arms. The pit bull started to bark and slobbered even more, but a firm hand grabbed his collar and lifted him up slightly to cut off his wind and silence him.

"I'll be with you in a moment," the vet said, smiling, before shutting the door again.

Mishima meowed faintly in relief.

When the pit bull and the skinhead came out, I picked up the cat carrier and went in. The vet seemed much more relaxed than she'd been at my place, perhaps because she was in her own territory.

"My name's Meritxell, by the way," she said, although I hadn't asked, as she took Mishima out of the carrier.

While she was injecting him, I studied her face. I once read somewhere that the beauty of a face isn't part of a particular cultural canon but a concept shared by all ethnic groups. Apparently, the same face would look attractive to the vast majority of human beings. Experiments have been run in nurseries, showing that babies have different reactions depending on the facial features of the staff member. They tend to cry when they see an unattractive face, while they are soothed by and will smile at one with regular features.

When she finished her work, Meritxell gave me another smile. That of course didn't mean she was going to accept an invitation to hot chocolate and ladyfingers. I opted for discretion and left without saying a word.

I saw a fleeting expression of disappointment on her face. No doubt she would have said no, but probably she would have loved me to ask her. I've never dared to probe too deep into the mysteries of female coquetry.

Seeking and Finding

Since I had the rest of the morning free, I thought I'd pay Titus a visit in the hospital.

During my Metro journey, I took the opportunity to read a few of Buddha's aphorisms, which could be used for the book. I felt a bit embarrassed pulling out the anthology I'd found in Titus's apartment. That car full of gray faces didn't seem to be the best place for contemplative reading. Soon, however, I realized that no one was paying attention to what I or anyone else was doing. All the passengers looked on without seeing, with their eyes open—which is worse than them having their eyes closed. In that case, they could dream.

This reminded me of a passage I'd particularly liked from Pessoa's *The Book of Disquiet*. In it, Pessoa says, more or less, that when we're asleep we all become children again because, as we slumber, we can do no wrong and are unaware of life. By some kind of natural magic, the greatest criminal and the most callous egotist become holy during their sleep. Therefore, according to the poet, there is hardly any difference between killing a sleeping man and a child.

From *saudade*—another untranslatable term—

in Portuguese, I jumped to the words attributed to Siddhartha Gautama:

Pain is inevitable
but suffering is optional.

He who doesn't know what to attend to
and what not to heed
attends to the unimportant
and ignores the essential.

That's me. I got off at the Hospital Clínic stop, almost angry that someone who lived twenty-five hundred years ago should be giving me advice.

"How are your two missions going?" Titus asked.

"I've finished the contents page for the book. What's the other mission?"

"Finding Gabriela, of course."

"So far I've drawn a blank in my search."

"I didn't tell you to search for her, but to find her," Titus pointed out.

"I don't see the difference."

"While you're looking, your eyes can go no further than the limits of your expectations. It would be like me looking for God under the bed because, in my position, that's the most comfortable thing. Do you understand?"

I nodded, thinking again about the drunk man looking for his keys next to the lamppost.

"So," Titus added, "when you're looking, you never find anything really important."

"What am I supposed to do, then? Hang around with my arms crossed?"

"On the contrary," Titus said, sitting up in his bed.

"In order to find something," he went on, clutching my hand, "you've got to let yourself go. If you follow preconceived ideas, you won't even see what's happening in front of your nose."

I nodded again and noticed that the other bed was empty.

"What happened to your roommate?" I asked. "Where's he gone?"

"If I knew," Titus said with a sad smile, "they'd give me the Nobel Prize for Everything."

"The difficult I'll do right now / The impossible will take a little while"

The assignment on Kafka's *The Castle* was revealing, if only because it demonstrated that the students had not understood a thing about it.

This has always been my favorite novel by Kafka, maybe because it's the most enigmatic. Since he died when it was only half finished, one can only guess what would have happened in the end to the land surveyor K., who is constantly thwarted in his attempts to reach the castle.

Was Gabriela my personal castle? Worried by this association, I brushed up on the basic plot on my way to the bar with the terrace.

The land surveyor K. is wandering around, confused by a series of contradictory signs:

> K. arrives in a snowbound town, where he's been summoned by the castle owners.
>
> Once he has found shelter at the inn, a telephone call informs him that he will never be able to go to the castle.
>
> Shortly afterward, he receives a letter confirming that he has been employed in the service of the lords of the castle.
>
> The mayor informs K. that the castle has

no need for land surveyors and an administrative error is the cause of the confusion.

The very same day a letter tells him that the inhabitants of the castle are very satisfied with his surveying work.

Although he receives this message, K. is still unable to do his work, and all his attempts to reach the castle fail.

The castle is an emblem of all the most absurd human aspirations—such as the desire for immortality or my efforts to rekindle an old love from thirty years ago. This thought took me back to Titus once more. He'd told me that if I went looking for Gabriela I wouldn't find her, but I wanted to try again, one last time.

I decided that if the madman was sitting on the terrace I'd walk past and never go back. All the tables were free, as it was a cold, windy day, so I sat down at the one in the middle and, once again, asked for a vermouth. I rubbed my hands, trying to get some warmth into them, realizing as I did so that I seemed to be irresistibly attracted to the terrace, like the moon to the earth. I was a ridiculous satellite spinning around an impossible dream.

I studied the to-ing and fro-ing of all the passersby going in both directions. If Gabriela was there among all those people, it would have been like finding a needle in the proverbial haystack, but still I wanted to give it one final chance.

I was humming to the music drifting out of the bar—Billie Holiday crooning "The difficult I'll do right now / The impossible will take a little while"—when a sinister figure loomed before me so fast I had no time to react. The bearded man sank into the metal chair and placed his manu-script on the table.

I could have finished my vermouth and left. Yet I felt inexplicably rooted to my seat. Feeling strangely calm, I kept watching the passersby.

Something's going to happen today.

There was no reason for thinking this, but an arrow had pierced the layers of my unconscious to tell me. Perhaps that's why I wasn't too startled when the man in the hat asked, "Do you feel nostalgia for the future?"

A Successful Failure

I studied the man's round face—his beard, his mustache, his protruding lower lip.

"I can't feel nostalgia for something that hasn't happened," I said.

"Can't you?" he replied, pulling his chair closer to mine, without leaving his table. "We all know more or less what's going to happen, because to a great extent we choose our futures. This is a trick used by good soothsayers."

"What do you mean?"

"Reading the future is like playing chess. An average player can predict the next two or three moves on the board. A good player, many more. It's a question of logic and coherence."

"And you've been able to see where your game's heading?"

"Yes. Before the checkmate there are some great adventures. That's why I'm nostalgic for the future. It will be wonderful, and I'd like to be there already."

"Well, since it depends on you," I said, humoring him, "can't you bring the game forward?"

"That's impossible. You have to go through lots of things before that, you understand? In chess, some moves lead to the next ones. If you interfere with the game, nothing will happen at all."

"Let me guess, then. The future for which you feel nostalgia is written in this manuscript you're always carrying around with you."

"You're a clever boy," he said with a grimace. "Perhaps you can help me with something."

"Uh-oh. Houston, we have a problem," I said with a laugh.

"April 11th, 1970."

"What?"

"The date when they launched *Apollo 13*. A bad number. It almost cost them their lives."

"I see you're superstitious."

"You have to be when the signs are so clear. *Apollo 13* was launched at 13:13 on a date whose numbers add up to thirteen. Try it: 4/11/70."

"That doesn't prove anything."

"It was a miracle they made it back to earth. That's why NASA called the mission a 'successful failure.' Beautiful definition, don't you think?" He gave me a conspiratorial glance and drained his coffee.

"So what's today's move, then?" I said.

"To discover who wrote a piece of music I like a lot. Do you know anything about music?"

"A fair bit," I confessed.

"Good," he said, brightening up. "Then perhaps you can help me. I was watching a film yesterday on TV. It was about two vampires locked in an apartment in New York."

"Were the vampires Catherine Deneuve and David Bowie?"

"I think so. Sometimes you could hear some very sad music played on the piano. I'd like to know who wrote it. I couldn't see it in the credits."

"I think it's a piece by Ravel—'Le Gibet,' or something like that. The gibbet. Not a very cheerful title."

"Indeed. But thanks for the information."

He stood up, left a coin on the table, and tipped his hat.

"Valdemar's leaving."

And he headed off in the direction he'd come from, with his manuscript under his arm.

Venetian Boat Song

I finished my vermouth and sat there pensively until the freezing wind persuaded me to leave.

Ravel's languid chords were echoing in my head, and I now wanted to hear the piece again. I checked my watch. If I hurried I could get to the music shop before it closed.

This was a small establishment in Carrer Tallers specializing in classical music. I hadn't been there for over a month. If there was anywhere one could find a recording of Ravel's "Le Gibet," this was the place.

I recklessly dashed across Carrer Pelai, took a shortcut down Carrer Jovellanos, and reached the shop five minutes before it closed for lunch. I walked past the drowsy cashier and was greeted by a delightful melody. I hadn't heard it for ages. It was one of Mendelssohn's *Songs without Words* titled "Venetian Boat Song," a piece for the piano, like Ravel's, but full of lyricism.

I decided to leave "Le Gibet" for the time being and went automatically from the Contemporary Music section to the Romantics. Before looking for the recording I intended to take home with me, I closed my eyes and waited for the last notes of "Venetian Boat Song" to fade out. When I opened my eyes, my heart began to thump so hard I nearly fainted. There, on the other side of the display, was Gabriela.

Although we were only a few inches apart—I could even smell the fragrance of her long wavy hair—she hadn't seen me. She was blinking as she was looking for something on one of the shelves.

Fighting off the panic attack that was pushing me to run away, I held my breath, waiting for Gabriela to look up.

When she did, my heart began pounding like a war drum. I had a few instants to admire the constellation of freckles on her cheeks before she shot me an inquisitive glance.

My first move was not the most imaginative.

"Hello."

A look of perplexity passed across her face. That was hardly surprising. I, too, felt as if I was in a daze, and I'd just broken the ice in the clumsiest way.

"Do you remember me?"

She stared at me with her almond-shaped eyes and said, "No. What do you want?"

I was so thrown by her response that I hesitated before I continued. If the whole thing was just an illusion and I'd recognized her but she didn't remember me, I'd be making a complete fool of myself. Yet I forged ahead. "I think we used to play hide-and-seek together many years ago in a neoclassical mansion on the right side of La Rambla and—"

"I have no idea what you're talking about." She seemed alarmed. "You must have the wrong person."

With that, she turned around and took refuge in another part of the shop.

Blushing with shame, I left the shop with no music apart from the jangling fragments of my broken heart.

A Magic Lantern

Trying to find something to distract me, I began
to mull over what I now considered to have
been the weirdest afternoon of my life. After
The Castle and my chat with Valdemar, I'd
chanced upon Gabriela, who hadn't even
recognized me.

Why, then, had she shot me such a knowing
glance at the traffic light? Not only that, she'd
turned around to give me one last look before
continuing on her way. Or had the whole thing
been nothing more than a fever-induced halluci-
nation?

On my way home, I replayed the scene in the
music shop in my mind. I finally came up with
the only logical explanation. Our eyes had just
happened to meet when we were crossing the
road, and she'd turned around by chance. We all
turn around sometimes when we're walking on
the street.

Without a doubt, she was the same person
who'd roused my passions thirty years earlier
with a butterfly kiss. The problem was that she
did not remember it. Maybe this scene from our
childhood had meant nothing to Gabriela—not
then and certainly not now.

For the first time I accepted the painful fact

that I was not a memorable man. The worst, most absurd thing was that I was hopelessly in love with her.

When I got home I almost rushed out again to the hospital to tell Titus what had happened. Don't they say that a sorrow shared is a sorrow halved?

I decided against it. I had accepted defeat and didn't want to rub salt into my own wounds. In order to alleviate my sorrows I'd do the only thing I knew how to do: work. As I went upstairs laden with books, I was glad that I had this extra task to keep me busy.

After my obligatory pause in front of the *Wanderer*, I sat down at Titus's desk ready to get on with the job.

I'd pasted the titles from the contents page on separate pages of the document with the intention of filling up each section with whatever ideas occurred to me. I glanced at the final section, "Love in Lowercase," and added another detonator of universal love.

No. 2: Talk to a Stranger

I had to include this because my conversation with Valdemar had taken me to the topic of Ravel, which led me to the music shop. There, the "Venetian Boat Song" had carried me away, along mysterious canals, to Gabriela. But what good had it done me?

I briefly abandoned this section in order to work on "Heart in the Hand." While rereading *Werther* before one of my classes, I'd come across a passage in which Werther offers his friend some moving thoughts on the mysteries of love. He'd included an anecdote. Full of self-pity, I began to copy it out:

Wilhelm, what is the world to our hearts without love? What is a magic lantern without light? You have only to kindle the flame within, and the brightest figures will shine on the white wall; and, if love only shows us fleeting shadows, we are yet happy when, like mere children, we behold them and are transported with the splendid phantoms. I have not been able to see Charlotte today. I was prevented by a social occasion from which I could not disengage myself. What was to be done? I sent my servant to her house, that I might at least see somebody today who had been near her. Oh, the impatience with which I waited for his return! The joy with which I welcomed him! I should certainly have caught him in my arms and kissed him, if I had not been ashamed.

It is said that the Bonona stone, when

placed in the sun, attracts its rays and for a time appears to glow in the dark. So it was with me and this servant. The idea that Charlotte's eyes had dwelt on his countenance, his cheek, his very apparel, endeared them all inestimably to me, so that at the moment I would not have parted from him for a thousand crowns. His presence made me so happy! Do not laugh at me, Wilhelm. Can that which makes us happy be a delusion?

III

The Pathos of Things

The Gondolier Again

A week after that strange, sad afternoon, there was another sign. I was free that morning, so I set about some housework and tuned in to the classical-music station on the radio.

I was washing a pile of food-encrusted plates when the announcer mentioned *Songs without Words*. I turned off the tap and turned up the volume, waiting to discover some hidden message.

". . . In 1828, the composer gave his favorite sister Fanny a birthday present, a piece he called 'Song without Words.' Mendelssohn was nineteen years old at the time. Throughout his career he kept adding more short piano pieces to it. The first collection of *Songs without Words* was published in 1832. It was very successful among the middle classes of the period, since they were starting to install pianos in their living rooms and these short works were very much to their taste. Although the piano pieces were untitled, Mendelssohn's Victorian admirers, convinced that the musical miniatures had some kind of storyline, began to give some of them pretentious names such as 'Lost Happiness,' and others nonsensical ones such as 'The Bee's Wedding.' Mendelssohn himself contributed to this by naming some of his *Songs without Words*—for example, such well-known pieces as 'Venetian Boat Song,' which we shall now listen to."

Here we go again. I closed my eyes to take in the song, paying close attention.

Yet—and this was the strangest thing—I didn't recognize it. The melancholy piece I had been listening to in Gabriela's presence had been replaced by another, much slower and more solemn, although equally beautiful song.

This was certainly not the gondolier I remembered. Either the announcer was mistaken or I'd been tricked into confusing a bee getting married with a gondolier—or something like that. Yet another mystery to add to my personal archive.

When the song ended, I started to vacuum the rug as Mishima, hissing and making sideways leaps, took on the noisy machine.

"We're going to have a chat tomorrow," I told him. "You're going to help me with the chapter on feline philosophy."

Once I was done with my household chores, I basically had three options: stay at home reading, go upstairs to Titus's place, or go out. I checked my watch and saw that it was after midday.

The perfect time for a vermouth. I headed off to the bar. I hadn't been there for a week.

However, once I'd ventured beyond the bounds of Gràcia, I thought I should go and see Titus.

I hadn't spoken to him since my encounter with Gabriela and had to face up to the painful task of telling him what had happened. That was probably the very reason I'd been avoiding him, taking refuge in my classes and writing Francis Amalfi's book.

Since all the cleaning had left me exhausted, I took a taxi so I could rest a little on the way to see my friend and confidant.

The driver was a broad-shouldered man with gray hair pulled back in a ponytail, in the style of an American Indian. Like many taxi drivers, he was a chatty fellow and, after I'd told him where I wanted to go, he gave me an update on the latest news.

"A ninety-year-old woman received a letter dating from 1937. That just goes to show you the speed of our postal services, eh?"

"Really?" I said, trying to sound interested.

"That's what I heard. Her boyfriend wrote it from the Ebro front. He died on the battlefield, so you could call it a letter from beyond the grave."

"What did the old lady say?"

"She cried a lot. That's to be expected: it must have brought back memories."

"I guess so."

"And it's not the first time something like this has happened," the taxi driver added. "A few years ago they found a whole sack of letters that had been sitting in a cellar for ages. The director of the postal service had to issue a statement in order to avoid a scandal."

"What did he say?"

"Some nonsense like, 'No need to worry: there weren't any love letters in the bag.'"

Dramatic Effect

When I arrived at the hospital, Titus's bed was empty. They informed me that he had been taken out for some tests. I wanted to wait, but the buxom nurse insisted that I should leave.

"He'll need some rest after this."

This reminded me of Valdemar's space explorations, so I headed off to the bar. As I was walking through l'Esquerra de l'Eixample, I wondered how he made a living. It was hard to imagine him having a serious job of any kind, although his clothes suggested that he wasn't short of money. If he wasn't living off an inheritance, he had to be doing something.

When I got to the crossroads, I saw that Valdemar had just gotten up from his table and was picking up his manuscript, about to leave. I caught up with him just as he was striding away to wherever he was going.

"Did you find the piece by Ravel?" I asked him for the sake of starting a conversation.

"I'm not looking for it," he responded very brusquely. "You told me it was called 'Le Gibet.' That's all I needed to know."

"So you only wanted to know the name of the piece?"

"Yes, I like calling things by their names. Don't you?"

As we walked down one side of the Plaça de Catalunya, I remembered the mystery of Mendelssohn's gondolier and told Valdemar about it.

"Favor for favor," he answered without slowing down. "Take me to a music shop, and I'll clear up the mystery for you. I'm very good at reading CD cases."

I led him to the classical-music shop, and we got there a few minutes before closing time. We were already halfway through the door when, acting on impulse, I pulled Valdemar back onto the street. He wasn't in the least surprised by my behavior, and we continued striding along together.

"I've had enough of music," I said. "Can I take you to lunch? I know a good restaurant not far from here."

He nodded slightly. I was trying to slow down my heart, which was racing madly after I'd seen Gabriela inside the shop again.

When We Go to the Moon

I led the way through the maze of alleys to the Romesco, a small restaurant I'm quite fond of in the Raval neighborhood. Valdemar didn't say a word all the way there, which gave me the opportunity to try to make sense of what was happening.

Then it hit me, and I laughed at myself for not having seen it earlier. It was no miraculous coincidence that Gabriela had reappeared in the music shop. Of course! She worked there.

This realization was comforting in a way, because now I knew where to find her. I didn't need to go back to sitting on the terrace on the off chance she'd walk by. I only had to go to the shop. Yet this didn't help me with the main problem—namely, that Gabriela hadn't recognized me or been at all receptive to my reminiscences of our childhood. As far as she was concerned, I was a stranger, and the most intimate interaction I could hope for between us was my purchasing a CD from her. And that was exactly what I decided to do.

We managed to grab the only unreserved table in the restaurant before a horde of low-budget tourists swarmed through the whole place. They serve simple dishes there, so I asked for salad and fish for both of us, plus a bottle of white wine.

"I don't have much time," Valdemar said.

"They're very quick here. Don't worry. Where do you have to go?"

"I have to get back to my research."

He tasted the wine, his index finger drumming on the thick manuscript that lay on the table. He then wiped his mouth with the napkin and announced, "A marvelous future is in store for humanity."

At first I didn't know what to say. As if I was experiencing a new déjà vu, I had the feeling that this wasn't the first time I'd heard such nonsense.

Then I said: "Now, that's certainly an optimistic viewpoint. But what's that got to do with the book?"

"A lot. I'm working on this book because I haven't been able to do anything else since I started feeling nostalgia for the future."

"You've talked about this before. You know where you'll be at some point in the future, but you can't see the moment you'll get there because that will be incredible. Am I right? But what's it got to do with the moon?"

Valdemar stabbed a morsel of white fish with his fork, lifted it up, and inspected it carefully before inserting it into his mouth. Then he said, "The book's been through several mutations. It might even be incorrect to call it a book, because by that we understand a finished, closed object. This is something else. It's a monster that keeps getting bigger and more and more deformed as new paths keep opening up. Let's call it destiny. Let's call it life."

"Does the title *The Dark Side of the Moon* refer to the huge rocky mass up there in the sky, or is it symbolic?"

"Both." There was a flash of enthusiasm in his eyes. "Let's say I started out with a purely scientific inquiry but then it branched out to other levels."

"So, are you a physicist?"

"Something like that. I'm a selenologist, but they kicked me out of academia. I began to have problems with my colleagues because of a theory I came up with. Scientists are a conservative bunch. You get the impression they're searching for truth, but in reality they're afraid of discovering any-thing beyond the limits of what they're prepared to accept. They prefer to close their eyes."

"Did you see something? What was your theory?"

"Well, actually, it was no more than a sup-position, a working hypothesis. I came to the conclusion that people don't age on the moon."

"What was the basis of your conjecture?" I was fascinated. "I mean, nobody's ever lived on the moon. Astronauts have been there only very briefly, right?"

"So they say. You've hit the nail on the head, Samuel. At the time, I was trying to demonstrate that there is a direct relationship between cellular oxidation and the earth's gravity. When I began to study the data collected by the various lunar missions, I began to doubt that any human being had ever set foot on the moon. I found too many gaps in the information. This would explain the fact that, despite the vastly superior technology we have nowadays, there have been no more trips to the moon. Unfortunately, I wasn't able to prove anything, because these missions either didn't happen in reality or their results were so insignificant that they might as well have not existed."

"How long have you been interested in the moon?"

"Since I was a little boy, when I dreamed of going there. In the sixties we were convinced that everyone would be able to travel to the moon in a couple of decades. That's why I feel I've been hoodwinked."

"Yet you're still going on about a marvelous future."

"Because I've realized that we'll get there in the end. There'll be a cataclysm on earth, and we'll have no choice but to colonize the moon. Then we'll discover that we're immortal. Happy ending."

House of Mirrors

After lunch, Valdemar took off into his own world, and I was left with the bill and two hours to kill before the music shop opened again.

Faced with a bunch of ravenous people who wanted my table, I got up without knowing where I should go with all my troubles. Wanting to avoid the masses of people pouring down La Rambla, I stayed in the Raval, wandering past Pakistani-owned international-call shops and video-rental stores.

On autopilot, I ended up at Marsella, a beautiful but run-down bar I hadn't been to since my student days. It had been my favorite then because of the mirrors covering all its walls and its bohemian atmosphere.

I went inside out of pure nostalgia, and to check that there'd been no major changes. But it still had the same scruffy mirrors, hoary old bottles covered in dust, ancient posters with warnings to customers: SINGING IS PROHIBITED and NO PARKING.

Sitting at one of the many tables that were free at that hour, I remembered that I'd read somewhere that this was Barcelona's oldest café. A waiter with a South American accent brought me a coffee.

I checked the time. Half past three. In just over an hour I'd see Gabriela again. The mere thought of it made my hands break out into a cold sweat and my pulse race.

Seeing her again earlier today had been almost physically painful, and at the same time I had experienced a feeling of vertigo, as if I were about to fall into an abyss and she was the only thing I could cling to. Right then, I thought I'd die of grief if I had to give her up.

As I was pondering all this and getting a bit teary, I saw that an old drunk at the next table was observing me with a maternal expression as she smoked her rank cigarettes. She was coughing between drags, but I could see in her eyes the empathy of someone who has consumed all her passion and is finally free.

Just then, the waiter came over to her table with the house special, a glass of diluted absinthe with a burning sugar cube. The old woman stopped looking at me to concentrate on the flames.

The scene reminded me of a book of poems by Bukowski. He's never been one of my favorite authors, but I believe he deserves a place of honor in world literature just for the title of the collection:

BURNING IN WATER, DROWNING IN FLAME.

Chinaski and Company

I gulped down what remained of my coffee and left Marsella feeling jittery, planning to wander around for a while and think about what to do when I saw Gabriela. I came to the conclusion that the best course of action would be to tell her I was sorry for my idiotic babbling—which essentially amounted to apologizing to her for the fact that she hadn't recognized me—and then behave like a regular customer.

In order to take my mind off that scene and the anguish its memory provoked, I started thinking once more about Bukowski, a German who'd landed in the United States in the early years of Nazism. I'd never really liked the grotty adventures of his alter ego Chinaski, but on reading an anecdote about him I discovered what a great man he was.

Once, when he was traveling by train along the West Coast, a small boy sitting next to him looked at the ocean and said, "It's not pretty." Bukowski shivered and thought the child was a genius because he'd never noticed this before.

Right from the moment of our birth we are made to think that the sea is pretty without being allowed to decide for ourselves.

I was walking along, lost in thought, when

someone tugged at my sleeve. Emerging from my daydream, I saw a young man dressed in a djellaba. He was in a phone booth, and he was holding the receiver in his other hand.

"There's still some money left," he said.

"What?"

"It's still got thirty cents. If I hang up, the phone company will get them, and I don't want them to. Come on, call your girlfriend."

He gave me the receiver and walked away, whistling. I didn't even have time to thank him. Since I didn't have a girlfriend, or any friends for that matter, I had to think about whom I could call in order to not waste the man's kind thought.

I remembered that I'd jotted down the number of the Hospital Clínic in case I needed to speak to Titus and decided to use the call to find out how his tests had gone.

After being put on hold for almost two minutes, I heard his cavernous voice on the other end of the line.

"I'm fine. You don't have to worry about me. How's the book going?"

Damn. The truth was that I'd written very little, so I quickly changed the subject, launching into a summary of recent events.

"I met this man," I told him. "His name is Valdemar, and he sounds like you when he talks about science."

"Must be a sign of the times," Titus remarked. "And what about Gabriela?"

"I tracked her down at last. She works in a music shop. But I don't stand a chance. She doesn't remember me."

"That doesn't matter. For the time being, just go and buy some records. You know what they say—"

But I didn't find out what they say, because the money ran out and the call was cut off. I searched my pockets for coins, but I only had ten cents, not enough for a local call.

I left the phone booth none the wiser and went on my way, as agitated as a soldier going off to the front.

Songs

They say that just before the curtain rises even the best actors go through a moment of excruciating tension that evaporates as soon as the play begins.

Something similar happened when I reached my destination. All of a sudden I felt calm, ready to rummage through the CDs like any other classical-music lover. Borne along by the strains of a very slow string quartet, I went to "M" for Mendelssohn in order to solve the mystery of the gondoliers.

I knew she was there, but my tactic was to focus all my senses on that section as if my life depended on it. Nonetheless, I couldn't help feeling apprehensive when I noticed Gabriela gliding toward me like a gentle shadow. As I flipped quickly through the CDs, I saw out of the corner of my eye that she was watching me with a faint smile on her lips. I turned toward her. I'd decided to play the part of a customer who is irritated at not being left to browse in peace. But, the moment we were face-to-face, the words that came out of my mouth were not at all those I had in mind.

"I'm sorry about the confusion the other day . . ."

"Don't worry," she said, smiling. "Can I help you at all?"

You have no idea.

I had to stick to my script.

"I'm looking for something you were playing here last week. It's one of the piano pieces from *Songs without Words*. I thought it was 'Venetian Boat Song,' but now I'm not so sure."

"Which one?"

"So there's more than one?" I was trying to put on an appearance of calm, which was completely at odds with my actual state of mind.

"There are three or four songs by Mendelssohn with that name."

"Well, I'd like to get acquainted with all those gondoliers." I was trying to be funny. "Which version would you recommend?"

Gabriela carefully flipped through the CDs. I took the opportunity to admire her long, dark, beautifully wavy hair, with highlights so black they were almost blue.

Finally she said, "There are two very good versions: the whole set by Barenboim and a selection played by András Schiff."

"I'll take the Barenboim. I'd like to have all the songs."

"We don't have it in stock at the moment. I've got only the Schiff recording." She handed me the CD, which had a photo of a rosy-cheeked man and the title *Lieder ohne Worte.*

I held it in my hands for a few seconds, wondering what to do. I wanted to take the songs home, but if I did that, I'd be throwing away the chance of seeing her again. There was a compromise solution that would end up costing me twice as much.

"I'd like both versions," I said. "Can you order the Barenboim for me, please?"

"Of course. It should arrive within a few days, and we'll let you know when we have it. Could you give me your telephone number, please?"

I gave it to her, ridiculously pleased that she should have it. Although it was only to inform me that the CD had arrived, in my dreams it had become a lovers' tryst.

"I'll see you in a few days," she said, smiling. Then she disappeared into the storeroom at the back of the shop.

I was spellbound. "See you."

Mono no aware

It doesn't matter. There I was, all alone in my apartment, making some coffee and repeating this.

"That's precisely the problem," I informed Mishima, who seemed to be listening attentively. "It doesn't matter because for her I don't exist."

I flopped on to the couch as the last light of the afternoon disappeared from my living room. With a heavy heart, I looked at the shelves full of books, the hi-fi system, the posters with portraits by Brassaï, the reading lamp that hadn't been turned on yet . . .

I wasn't up to listening to the CD I'd just bought. I was haunted by the Japanese notion of *mono no aware*—the pathos of things, a term that was beginning to pervade my being, very much against my will.

I remained there in the gloom for several minutes, until I finally decided to switch on the light, whereupon Mishima gave an approving meow. I picked up Rheingold's dictionary from the coffee table, longing to wallow in melancholy and knowing full well what I was doing.

The expression in question didn't feature in the dictionary itself but in a clipping I'd slipped inside it. It seems that it was used for the first time by the eighteenth-century Japanese poet Motoori Norinaga, who was referring to an extreme sensibility to things and an unfiltered relationship in which the observer merges with what is being observed, like the lover inhabiting the heart of his beloved.

This profound experience breeds melancholy, a condition that would seem to be inherent to the world's substratum. It's all about beauty and sadness. This is the title of a novel by Yasunari Kawabata, Japan's first winner of the Nobel Prize in Literature.

Maybe everything that is beautiful is sad because it's so ephemeral, like a butterfly kiss.

Fed up with myself, I closed the book and went to wash the dishes. I'd been insufferably romantic lately.

As I was running hot water over a plate, I could see the moon, full and splendid in the sky. I thought it looked very lonely up there. A good reason for going to visit.

Perhaps Valdemar was right in thinking that our immortality resided there. But who would want to spend eternity on the moon?

Siddhartha's Candles

On Saturday morning I woke up feeling more upbeat. We're never alone, and the idea that we are is just another human illusion.

The sight of the moon had provoked some kind of reaction within me during the night, because I was giddy with the euphoria of a man who believes that anything is possible. The scenes of the previous day that had made me sad were now cause for optimism. Was I going mad?

The sun had woken Mishima, who was doing his early-morning stretching exercises, yawning at the same time.

I leaped out of bed, fired by the conviction that I was the master of my own fate. I therefore had nothing to fear, not even Mendelssohn. I put on the CD of the *Songs* and ransacked my pantry to make myself an abundant breakfast.

To my delight I discovered that the version by András Schiff was the one they'd been playing in the shop. It was just the tonic I needed in order to summon up Gabriela and dream of enchanting scenes. Only magic could take me back to a fleeting childhood love that had lasted only as long as the flutter of an eyelid.

The first gondolier reminded me of Gabriela's smile, the constellation of freckles sprinkled over her cheeks, her almond-shaped eyes. The very best of life—the wonders of the world—all brought together in one woman's face.

To an outside observer I would have looked like a half-wit daydreaming over a solitary Saturday-morning breakfast. True. Apart from Mishima, I was as alone as ever. But my solitude now seemed to be densely populated.

I went over the love-in-lowercase succession of events which had unleashed my wild, crazy hopes: saucer of milk > cat > Titus > train track (curve) > Gabriela > terrace > Ravel > Mendelssohn > Gabriela > Titus (tests) > terrace > Valdemar > Mendelssohn (two gondoliers?) > Gabriela . . .

Where was this chain of cause and effect taking me? What about the moon? What was the moon doing in all of this?

There seemed to be a direct correlation between my opening up to the outside world—Mishima, Titus, and Valdemar, without forgetting my sister and her husband—and Gabriela's triple appearance. Would she be my reward for trying to help some strangers who had nothing to do with me?

Maybe the only people worthy of love are those who love indiscriminately, without denying to some what they give to others.

This idea took me to something I'd read before going to bed, an aphorism attributed to Siddhartha

Gautama. I went to get my little book in order to reread it.

Gondolier number two had appeared on the scene, and then I found an answer to some of my questions:

> Thousands of candles can be lit by just one candle, and the life of that candle will not be shorter because of it. Happiness is never diminished by being shared.

Treatise on
Feline Philosophy

After a Saturday devoted to daydreams and finishing some university work—namely, preparing my classes for the coming week—on Sunday I started to feel some pangs of conscience concerning Francis Amalfi's book.

After agreeing to do the job for Titus, I'd barely managed to produce ten pages: the fragment from *The Sorrows of Young Werther*, a few aphorisms from Buddha, the section on love in lowercase—and that was about it. *A Short Course in Everyday Magic* needed a breakthrough moment in order to convince me I was capable of finishing it.

I glanced at Mishima. He was on the couch looking bored, like a typical human being. Before I succumbed to my customary Sunday-afternoon depression, I went up to Titus's apartment with him in order to grapple with the chapter on "Feline Philosophy."

I turned on Titus's laptop and started collecting material. There were quite a few manuals on cats in Titus's library, and one of them was tailor-made for me. It was called *Ten Spiritual Lessons You Can Learn from Your Cat*. The author, Joanna Sandsmark, said in her introduction that her two cats had taught her to land on her feet and to purr when happy.

That wasn't a bad start, but I needed to look for something else.

I've always associated cats with having nine lives, so I decided that this would be a good starting point. Keeping Mishima in sight, I started to write, spurred on by a sudden burst of inspiration.

I. SPIRITUAL LIFE

Cats are great meditators besides being masters in the art of yoga. This member of the feline species can remain immobile for hours, traveling toward its own center, and then, in an instant, make the leap into the external world, focusing all its senses on what is happening there. Its vitality comes from this state of repose since the cat consumes no energy in intermediate states. It's either in action or at rest. When it acts, it does so as if its life depended on it. When it rests, it's as if it never had to get up again. It doesn't waste time dithering.

II. EMOTIONAL LIFE

Cats are said to be selfish, but in reality they're just smart. They won't come to you if they can make you go to them.

Their power resides in their apparent indifference. They prefer to let you love them than to put their feelings at risk by revealing them. Like the good Taoists that they are, they do without doing and rule without ruling. They limit themselves to keeping their dignity and acting according to their whims. They don't go looking for love and therefore obtain it without asking. Dogs have a master. Cats have servants.

III. A LIFE OF THE SENSES
A cat in your home is a reminder that you must always pay attention. We frequently miss opportunities because we are not aware of them. Cats refine their senses, monitor their surroundings, and are alert to the smallest change. Theirs is a serene alertness, full of active patience. While resting they are attuned to the people around them, ready to act when necessary. Thanks to this watchfulness, events tend to turn out in their favor.

I stopped there, impressed by what I had written.

Mishima was thumping the rug with his tail, urging me to get back to work. I mulled over other themes I could develop: a cat's hygiene, its ability to disappear before a disagreeable turn of events, its almost supernatural intuition . . .

The lesson was clear. I, too, had to be attentive from now on. I looked forward to the week ahead and realized that anything could happen. The secret lay in keeping my eyes wide open and leaping fearlessly when the time was right.

Breaking the Egg

The dance students' exams had started, which meant that the German literature seminar had been moved to the first lesson on Monday morning. This one was about Hermann Hesse and, in particular, his novel *Demian*, which he originally signed using the name of its main character, Emil Sinclair.

I entered my classroom to face my few, half-asleep students.

I got straight to the point. After a brief account of the main features of Hesse's biography, I handed out the themes from *Demian* I'd chosen to discuss and then focused on one part of the novel that seemed particularly significant.

Emil Sinclair has lost contact with his friend Max Demian, who'd revealed to him some of the more sinister aspects of the society in which he lived. One night Sinclair dreams that Demian is holding a coat of arms featuring a heraldic bird. The bird comes to life and starts to devour Demian's entrails.

Still affected by the dream, Sinclair decides to paint the bird as he dreamed it and sends it to his friend's old address. His reply arrives in a mysterious fashion, in the form of a folded piece of paper tucked into one of his school books. Demian's reading of the dream has taken the form of a revelation:

> The bird is fighting its way out of the egg. The egg is the world. Whoever wishes to be born must destroy a world. The bird is flying toward God.

At this point, the class know-it-all—wearing round glasses, just like Hesse—put up her hand.

"Hesse nicked that idea from Goethe."

"Did he, indeed?" I didn't like her tone.

"That's what it says here," she said, pointing at a German study guide with a yellow cover. "Goethe had previously mentioned breaking an egg in the diaries he wrote during his time in Italy."

"Well, I've also broken an egg or two to make myself an omelet, but you don't have to read Goethe or Hesse to do that."

I regretted my words as soon as they left my mouth. The student kept her composure and started to read aloud—with a perfect German accent—what Goethe had felt as he traveled around Italy. I rendered one of the sentences into Catalan for a slightly obtuse boy who always required simultaneous translation.

"He believed he was shedding a new shell every day and that he had been transformed down to the very marrow of his bones."

"You're right," I conceded. "They're both talking about the same thing. I suppose everyone has to break the egg sooner or later. What does this image mean to you?"

This resulted in the usual silence that followed my saying or asking something out of the ordinary. I turned to one timid boy who rarely opened his mouth. His response to my invitation to speak was a shrug.

Luckily for him, Miss Know-It-All entered the fray once again with an idea she had found in the introduction.

"Hesse talks of shedding old skins. So, in a sense, he was anticipating the egg."

"Bravo. What skins was he talking about?"

I could glimpse a flash of pride and sensitivity behind the girl's glasses.

"The skins of the soul."

The Album of Life

I didn't have any more classes till midafternoon, so I weighed my options: continue the work of Francis Amalfi, prepare my classes, or visit Titus.

I decided to go for an entirely different option, a new one. I'd go and visit my sister. She was usually at home in the mornings. She'd left her job recently, after being afflicted by a mysterious illness that no one had yet been able to identify.

Having decided to stick with the course of action I had adopted on the day of our Epiphany lunch, I started to repeat my mantra—*the opposite is best*—and hailed a taxi.

As I gave the driver the address, I noticed his broad back and gray hair pulled into a ponytail. I also saw that his eyes were staring at me from the rearview mirror. There was no doubt about it. This was the man who'd told about the mislaid sack of letters.

The doorman told me that Rita had gone out but that she'd be back soon.

I decided to wait for her inside the apartment. As soon as I opened the door with the key she'd given me in case of emergency, I was greeted by the same old smell of patchouli permeating the whole place. When I had lived there with my father and sister I'd never noticed it, but now I could easily recognize the smell of an unhappy childhood.

My first thought was to turn on the television, which is what Andreu does the moment he walks through the door. However, the bovine image of my brother-in-law made me change my mind, so I wandered around the apartment, an intruder making the most of being alone.

The living room and bedroom were constantly being redecorated, so there was nothing of interest there. Neither was there anything remarkable about the kitchen, where I found only some organic fruit juice and one bottle of vile-tasting beer from Malta.

My inspection of the apartment took me to the storage room, a long, narrow space full of bits of furniture shrouded with ghostly-looking sheets. I tried to turn on the light, but the bulb had blown, which suggested that no one had been in there for a while.

When my eyes got used to the feeble light filtering in from outside, I gingerly made my way to the back of the room. There I found a chest of drawers full of mementos from my childhood: school certificates, old comics, toys, and useless knickknacks. I groped around and found a big iron lamp which, surprisingly, lit up when I switched it on.

This discovery shed light—literally and metaphorically speaking—on other things that brought back memories and past suffering: handwriting exercise books, a compass, a game of Chutes and Ladders, the bracelets my sister used to make out of strands of plastic . . .

In the bottom drawer I found some music magazines and an old photo album I didn't recall having seen before. I opened it and shone the light onto the first page, where a large portrait of my father almost made me put the album right back where I'd found it.

After hesitating for a few moments, I opened it again with the morbid curiosity of an archaeologist digging into his own past. It began with a series of portraits of my father in different situations: at his university graduation ceremony, on a trip to London, or with my newborn sister in his arms.

The images stirred up bitter feelings in me. Sitting on the storage-room floor like I used to as a small boy, I remembered how I had neglected my father when he was dying. I was about twenty then and still felt the scars of a childhood full of impenetrable silences.

After my mother died, he disengaged completely from our lives, apart from the financial support he gave us. He thought he was doing his duty. My sister reacted by indulging in outrageous, extravagant behavior, while I plunged into a silence that answered his.

Resentment piled up in a stony carapace around my heart until I was as unfeeling as he was.

After my father died, I started to forgive him. I realized that he'd done all that he was capable of doing for us. I had no right to demand more than he could give.

It's so easy to make peace with the dead. I kept turning the pages of the album.

I came across myself at the age of three, dressed up as a football player. The next page had a black-and-white photo of my sister in her ballet class. She must have been about eight, and her raised leg was resting on the barre next to a large mirror. Behind her, a row of little girls, their heads held high, did their best to hold the position.

Then I saw her.

I could hardly breathe. Another ghost from the past. I saw Gabriela at the back of the room. Like all the other little girls, her leg was on the barre and her arm raised to form an arc. Unlike the others, however, her gaze wasn't lost in the effort to keep her balance. She was looking straight at the camera.

I carefully detached the photo. This was the little girl I'd met under the stairs. Like an adolescent worshipping an idol, I gently kissed the photo and put it in my pocket.

Platform World

I rushed to the bar as fast as I could. I needed to speak with somebody about what was happening, and Valdemar seemed to be the right person to talk to. But I soon realized that my mission was futile.

"You see that man in black sitting inside?" He asked me this in an enigmatic tone, pointing with his foot.

I glanced sideways. The man in question was a young redhead wearing a black jacket and trousers. He had just taken a sip of his beer.

"Yes. Who is he?"

"I don't know, but I'd like to find out."

I briefly suspected that Valdemar was attracted to the redhead, but he soon shot down that theory.

"That man is a great mystery," he added.

"What's so mysterious about him? He's just a guy having a beer in a bar."

"So it seems, but don't forget that, like the moon, people have a dark side. You'll see what I mean in a moment. Do you have a watch?"

I pulled up the sleeve of my jacket to demonstrate that I did. Valdemar nodded in approval.

"Take note, then: he's going to stand up at 1:24 exactly, and then he'll come out that door humming."

I looked at my watch. It was 1:21. Although I had no idea what this was all about, I was curious to see if Valdemar could foresee the future. We sat there, in tense silence, waiting for the minute hand to reach the predicted time.

Indeed, at 1:24 on the dot the redheaded man left a coin on the counter and walked out humming. I was mystified.

"How did you know that? Is this one of your chess moves?"

"No." He chuckled behind his beard. "Simple observation. He's been coming here for months, and he always does the same thing. No matter what time he gets here, he always stays exactly seventeen minutes, no more, no less. Then he leaves. I discovered this when I started timing him."

I couldn't decide who had the most screws loose: the person who was being timed or the one doing the timing.

"Do you know why he does that?" I asked.

"How would I know?" His tone was irate. "I'm a physicist and I stick with the facts—which in themselves are already quite disconcerting. When you start paying attention to what's going on around you, you discover that you've been blind to a whole world of signs. There's nothing soothing about that, I can assure you."

"You mean things like the seventeen-minute customer?"

"That's nothing, a mere trifle compared with what I know and wish I'd never found out."

His words made me think of the prologue to *The Dark Side of the Moon*—which, for the first time, wasn't on the table. I assumed it was inside his backpack under the table.

"What did you discover?"

"It all began on a Metro platform. I used to sit there every afternoon, as my doctor had prescribed."

"What? Which doctor?"

"I had to see a psychiatrist for several months because of an accident. But he didn't give me any medication: it was just behavioral therapy."

"I'm not following you. You had an accident?"

"Yes."

Valdemar paused for a few seconds, trying to decide whether to tell me or not. In the end he said, "I have relatives in Ushuaia in Argentina. It's the southernmost city in the world."

What on earth has this got to do with the Metro and the shrink? I kept my question to myself because I didn't want to interrupt him.

"When I was working at the university and had some money, I used to go there every winter, when it's summer there. Well, it's still cold, actually, as it's close to Antarctica. It's a wonderful place for exploring unspoiled landscapes, which is what I used to do during those vacations. I'd take the car to the end of the road and walk on from there with my camera. On one of these solitary excursions there was a one-hundred-foot precipice that I didn't see, and I fell over the edge."

"One hundred feet? Nobody would survive a fall like that."

"Usually not, but I was lucky because a tree broke my fall. I must've hit more than one branch before I landed on the ground. I regained consciousness hours later next to a frozen river. My arm was broken, my lip was split, and there was no way of getting back to the trail leading to the car. There was a one-hundred-foot-high natural wall separating me from the way back. The only thing I could do was to follow the river and hope to find some inhabited place. I walked for fifteen hours, managing to forget about the pain, but then I reached a massive waterfall that was impossible to cross. It was getting dark and the temperature had dropped to ten degrees below zero. I certainly wouldn't have survived the night in that place. I would have froze to death before anyone could find me. I was terrified. Suddenly, I saw a rescue boat that was searching for me in the distance. I began to scream like a madman, but they couldn't hear me over the noise of the waterfall. It was almost dark and I could see the boat moving away. Then I had an idea that one might describe as brilliant."

"What did you do?"

"Something very simple, which hadn't occurred to me before. Miraculously, my camera wasn't smashed, so I was able to fire off the flash a few times. They saw the signal and came to rescue me. It was incredible. It took me six months to recover. While I was trying to save my life I didn't feel a thing, but as soon as I got to the hospital I started howling with pain. They had to drug me and knock me out."

"That's not surprising," I said. "The adrenaline kept you totally focused on what you had to do, like a cat pouncing on its prey. But . . . what's all this got to do with the Metro platform?"

"When I returned to Barcelona I had bad attacks of claustrophobia, which can occur several months after a trauma. I kept having this feeling of dread, of being trapped under a wall of rock. This was a problem because I had to take the Metro to get to the university but didn't feel up to it."

"So you started seeing a behavioral psychiatrist?"

"Yes, I did. He told me I didn't need medication, so he devised a therapy of gradual exposure, which is very effective for dealing with phobias. It consisted of going down into the Metro and sitting on the bench with the waiting passengers. Only that. At first I had to do it for five minutes, or as long as I could bear being underground. I then kept gradually increasing the time until I could do it for half an hour. That was the day I got on the train and went to tell the psychiatrist I was cured."

"Happy ending."

"Not quite, because that was the first time I saw the dark side, not of the moon, but of people. If I hadn't discovered that, things would be a lot easier for me now. I realized that some people on the platform never got on the train. They just stayed there. In normal conditions I wouldn't have noticed this, because when you go underground it's to get a train."

"Perhaps they were cold and taking refuge there."

"No. It was summer and as hot as hell. The air-conditioning was never working in that station. I can't believe that anyone would stay down there for fun."

"What were they doing, then?"

"That's what I asked the psychiatrist. I told him what I'd seen. Do you know what he said?"

"What?"

"He said, 'Perhaps they're in therapy like you.'"

Alice in the Cities

When I reached my street, my head was pounding like a drum. As I was about to enter my building, I realized that, despite the cold, I didn't want to go home. All that was waiting for me there was a cat and tasks to deal with—both my own work and what I had to do for Titus.

Acting on a rebellious impulse, I pulled the key out of the lock, turned around, and walked off to the Verdi movie complex to see what they were showing.

I was amazed to discover that they were screening *Alice in the Cities*, my favorite of all Wim Wenders's films.

It's a very special kind of road movie. A German journalist, Philip Winter, is traveling the United States on an assignment for a magazine. He takes such a long time trying to find something to write about that his editor cancels the deal and Philip decides to return to Germany. At the airport he starts chatting with a young German woman with a nine-year-old daughter named Alice. Just before departure, the woman leaves the child in Philip's care, promising to meet up with them later, but she fails to appear. After they land, Philip rents a car and he and Alice set out to find the only relative the child has in Germany: her grandmother. But Alice can't remember her name or the town where she lives. The only clue she has is a photograph of a house that looks like millions of others in Germany, and could be anywhere. They set out on their desperate journey, showing the photo to people in every town, to no avail, as Philip's money runs out.

I was in an emotional state when I walked out, perhaps because I've always felt like Alice in the cities, a waif hoping to find warmth somewhere.

Before going home, I went to have a bite to eat in one of the many Lebanese restaurants in the neighborhood. I had a minibottle of wine and indulged in the fantasy that I was Philip Winter. I liked the man: he had a clear goal at least, which was to find the grandmother so he could free himself of the burden of the little girl. My goal was much less clear.

In the darkness of my living room I could see that my answering machine was flashing. I imagined that it was one of those messages urging one to change one's telephone or water company, or whatever.

But the voice in the message was deep and sweet. It said something wonderful.

"Hello. We have your Barenboim CD. You can come to get it when it's convenient for you. Thank you."

Prisoner of the Heart

I've got an ace up my sleeve, and my luck's going to change. It was seven in the morning, and I got out of bed with this thought. I had almost another hour to laze in bed and enjoy the remnants of my dream. But I was bursting with energy and wanted to start my day as early as possible.

Before having a shower, I hit the PLAY button on my answering machine once more so I could hear Gabriela's voice again. She sounded delicious, a combination of slightly husky and delicate. What a pity she was only talking about a CD by a Jewish pianist, but that could change anytime now because I had an ace up my sleeve. At least I thought I did.

After a tedious German-language class, I was free until the afternoon. Ready to risk everything, I didn't want to wait a moment longer before going to see her.

I didn't have to go inside, because Gabriela was in the shopwindow, hanging up a poster about some new release. Since she had her back to me, I could gaze at the mane of hair rippling over her red pullover. She was thirty-seven and her beige corduroys showed off a very slim figure.

When she first noticed I was looking at her—my nose was almost pressing against the glass—she looked slightly baffled, as if she didn't know what I was doing there, but then she must have remembered my CD because she stepped out of the shopwindow and beckoned me inside with a big smile.

After placing the double-CD box set of the Barenboim version on the counter, she asked, "Do you have children taking piano lessons?"

I was taken aback. "No. Why do you ask?"

"The *Songs without Words* are typical learner pieces."

"Oh, really?" I was embarrassed.

"They all have to learn at least one. I didn't get past 'Spinning Song.' "

"I don't have children," I told her.

Then, as often happens in such cases, I did the dumbest thing I could do at the worst possible time. Without any explanation, I pulled the photo out of my pocket and placed it on the counter. Gabriela gave me a quizzical look, without paying any attention to the photo. She was clearly wondering why I was showing her a picture of some little girls at a ballet class when I'd just told her I didn't have any children.

Anyway, having gotten to this point, the only thing I could do was to see it through to the end.

"That little girl at the back of the line, do you know who she is?"

Gabriela picked up the photo carefully, and the expression in her eyes changed from uneasiness to bewilderment. I think I even glimpsed a tear.

"That's me."

Piano Lesson

András Schiff plays the "Venetian Boat Songs" as if they are serious pieces to be performed in concert halls. His version is slow and decadent, and he uses the pedal to heighten their languor.

Barenboim's recording, however, is truer to the original spirit of the pieces. Listening to his version of the songs makes me think of parlors in which well-brought-up young ladies practice on their pianos.

Schiff's "Venetian Boat Songs" are extremely passionate and sentimental, as if he's about todie after every bar. The first piece lasts two minutes and forty-one seconds, while Barenboim's version of the same song takes only one minute and fifty-two seconds. The message is clear. Daddy's girl, who's trying to finish her class as soon as possible, races through the exercise because she wants her afternoon snack.

I believe I was having all these thoughts—as I switched CDs after each piece—in order to protect myself. It's easier to concoct theories about Mendelssohn's piano works than to face certain facts. I was probably trying to put off any analysis of what had happened in the shop as I hadn't had the time to digest it all. Because, once again, something completely unexpected had occurred.

"This is for you," I'd said to Gabriela, handing her the photo.

She was astounded. "For me, really?"

"You can keep it. I don't think my sister will notice it's gone."

Then came the bombshell.

"Well, can I invite you for coffee, as a way of saying thank you?"

I couldn't believe my ears, couldn't speak, until she added, "I'll be free tomorrow at two. Can you be here then?"

I nodded. That was all I could do. Well, I believe I also said, "I'll be here."

Moon Dust

Wednesday began with a jolt. I was so agitated that I'd hardly slept a wink all night, and when the alarm went off I jumped out of bed like a jack-in-the-box.

Oddly enough, Mishima didn't follow my lead. He was fast asleep on the bed.

"No problem," I told him. "If I were you, I'd do the same."

I showered and got dressed very quickly, although there was absolutely no reason to hurry. In the blink of an eye I was on the street, heading for the Metro station. It was quite a warm day, but with every step I took I was feeling colder and colder. An icy chill was moving up my legs and making my whole body tremble.

Then I realized that I wasn't wearing any shoes. I'd left home in my socks and gone too far to turn back and put some shoes on. I'd be late for my nine o'clock class, and the shoe shops didn't open till ten. What on earth could I do?

All of a sudden the sky went dark—as if there had been a solar eclipse—and a familiar buzzing sound resounded in the city, where I suddenly seemed to be the only person walking around.

· · ·

When I opened my eyes I was in bed. I switched off the alarm.

I'd just had what's called a "false awakening." You dream you're awake and doing exactly what you'd be doing if you really had woken up. You remain under the impression of being awake until some strange detail—like being on the street without your shoes on, or a solar eclipse, or a buzzing sound—tells you that this can't really be happening—at least not in the waking world.

The annoying thing is that, once you understand what's gone on, you have to get out of bed and start the entire process all over again.

After finishing my morning classes I had to wait only two hours before I would see Gabriela again. I started feeling nervous. Without knowing where I was going, I crossed the road.

I needed to find something to distract me until two o'clock came around. It was a little early, but there was a chance that Valdemar would be sitting on the terrace, so I headed in that direction, without giving it a second thought.

None of the tables were occupied. I sat at the middle one—I'm a creature of habit—and asked for my aperitif as I basked in the February sun.

I had hoped Valdemar would be there, so that

his talk of lunar studies and nostalgia for the future would transport me far away from myself—which is exactly what I needed. However, the appearance of a familiar figure provided an unexpected source of entertainment.

It was the man in black who, according to Valdemar, always spent seventeen minutes at the bar.

Since I had nothing better to do, I decided to find out for myself whether the previous confirmation of his theory had been pure chance and the whole story was the product of Valdemar's overheated imagination. When the man took his seat at the bar and asked for a beer it was 12:43 on the dot. That meant he had to leave at one o'clock. He'd made it easy for me.

I played the detective, monitoring his movements and keeping an eye on my watch. The redheaded man took a couple of sips of his beer, leafed through a sports paper, and lit a cigarette. He put it out half smoked, had another sip of beer, and kept reading listlessly. The seventeen minutes were about to end, but the man didn't seem to be in the slightest hurry.

When the minute hand was vertical, a sudden ringing noise made me jump. It was the phone at the bar.

As the waiter reluctantly answered, the man in black left a coin on the bar and rushed out, as if awakened by the ringing.

Seventeen minutes. It was true.

However, I started wondering whether the man would have done the same thing if the phone hadn't rung. But my musings were interrupted by another surprise.

"I think it's for you," the waiter said, handing me the cordless phone.

I was baffled. Who could possibly know I was there? And how did the waiter know who I was? He didn't even know my name. Two words from the caller, however, put an end to the mystery.

"Valdemar speaking."

Well, it couldn't have been anyone else. Yet I was surprised that he'd phoned instead of coming to the bar as he usually did at midday.

"Is something wrong?"

The noise in the background made his voice sound as if it was coming from another planet. After a moment's hesitation, he answered, "Yes."

"Could you give me a few more details?"

"Having some problems. But it's not something I can talk about on the phone."

"We can talk about it this afternoon. Here's my number—"

He cut me off. "I told you, I can't talk on the phone. Tell me where you live and I'll come to you."

I rather reluctantly gave him my address. Then I changed the subject. "You sound as if you're miles away, as if you're calling from the moon."

"In a way I am." His tone suddenly relaxed. "It's not quite time yet, but I'm preparing for the launch."

"What will life be like on the moon?" I welcomed this change of topic. "I mean, when we have to flee from Earth and discover that we are immortal and all that."

"Oh, there are a few technical glitches that have to be sorted out first. But nothing too serious."

"Are you talking about the journey itself?"

"No, all that's sorted. The technology's good enough to get us there. The problem is the regolith."

"Regolith? What on earth is that?"

"It's moon dust, which is caused by the impact of meteoroids. The particles are so abrasive that within a few days it had disabled the astronauts' instruments. That's why nobody's had the bright idea of building hotels on the moon."

"Because of the regolith?"

"Yes, it would corrode any building they might put up there. It's like having sandpaper every-where. The astronauts were saved by the asbestos in their space suits. Now there's a fantastic material . . ."

All of a sudden I realized that the waiter was standing in front of me with his arms crossed. "Hey man, you're hogging the phone. It's supposed to be for work purposes only."

Mustache in the Sky

I had fifteen minutes to walk a distance of less than a hundred yards, so I headed off to the music shop in slow motion.

I was strangely aware of details that I didn't usually notice: the smell of pasta boiling in a saucepan, a puddle shaped like a fish, the smudge on a baby's forehead, the murmuring sound of distant trees . . .

I stopped to look in the shopwindows, whiling away the time and aware of the butterflies in my stomach.

I reached my destination a little early, three minutes to two. Nevertheless, I entered the shop.

Gabriela was talking softly to a fat man, who was showing her a catalog. I stood behind her without saying anything. The cashier seemed to have left already.

Maybe I should have waited on the street—or the salesman was making her edgy—because Gabriela interrupted her conversation and said to me, "Wait for me at the café. I'll be there in a few minutes."

"Which café?"

"Do you know the Kasparo?"

"Yes, it's not far from here."

I didn't need to be asked twice and went off

to the famous Kasparo, a café with tables under an arcade in a quiet square.

It must have been ten years since I'd been there, but the atmosphere seemed more or less the same: young people who had aged prematurely because they wanted to live too fast, recycled old hippies, the odd sidetracked tourist who'd come across the place by chance.

It wasn't a particularly warm day, but there were a few solitary souls having the daily special outside.

I found a free table next to a column and hastened to strike the right pose: man waiting for the woman he loves; first date. It's difficult to seem natural in such a situation, so I asked for a coffee and looked up. Just then, two especially fluffy clouds came together to create a great big mustache in the blue sky.

I watched it for ages, as if I'd gone there with no other purpose but to observe clouds moving. When I emerged from my reverie—which had kept anxiety at bay—I looked at my watch and it was almost two thirty.

I started to panic. Somehow I knew what was at stake. I wasn't prepared for a world without Gabriela, or without the illusion of Gabriela at the very least.

I was getting increasingly desperate when I saw her approaching the square. I had a few seconds to enjoy the lightness of her step, her feet appearing to glide just above the ground. Her hips were swaying under a green woolen dress that showed off her curves. Before she reached my table, a gust of wind lifted her hair and swung it around across her lips. Gabriela deftly brushed it back and said, "I'm sorry to have kept you waiting."

She sat in the chair facing mine.

"Don't worry. I've been watching the clouds." *What a terrible way to start.* I was annoyed with myself but couldn't leave the matter at that because it would have sounded even worse. "Do you know what? While I was waiting for you two long clouds joined up to make a mustache in the sky."

Gabriela looked at me as if she had some kind of weirdo sitting across from her. Then she took a deep breath and, with an expression that had abruptly turned serious, asked, "What do you want from me? I don't even know who you are."

I was stunned into silence. I'd planned to tell her lots of things before confessing what I felt for her—that is, if I was capable of doing so. Now I was facing her final verdict without having been given a chance to submit a single piece of evidence.

"Well," I said, trying to sound offhand, "I discovered a photograph of you as a little girl, and I gave it to you. After that, you invited me to have coffee with you. That's why we're here, isn't it?"

"Of course. What I want to know is why you brought me the photo. It's just a coincidence that your sister went to ballet classes with me, so what's it to you? There are hundreds of strangers in our family photo albums, and we don't all run around trying to find them."

Damn it! She's not making it easy for me. My only chance was to resort to my university lecturer spiel in an attempt to keep her at the table. If she got up and left, all would be lost.

"I'll tell you if you'll just listen carefully for a couple of minutes. You and I met when we were six or seven. Something special happened between us, even if you don't remember it, so the little girl in the photo remained engraved in my memory all these years. When our paths crossed at the traffic light, I recognized you, and that made a huge impression on me. It doesn't often happen that you recognize someone you knew as a child. You looked at me twice, first as we passed and then when you reached the pavement on the other side, before you continued on your way. That led me to believe that perhaps you'd experienced something similar."

"It's true, I did look at you," she confessed, brushing her hand through her hair, "but not because I remembered anything special. It was because you were walking around the streets in your pajamas."

"How did you notice that?" I suddenly felt

embarrassed. "I had my trousers and overcoat on top of them."

"It was easy to spot because your coat was open. That's why I turned around to look again." Now she smiled for the first time.

"Then the whole thing's been a misunderstanding." I was crushed. "But the photo proves that you are the person I remembered. Even if you don't recall what happened, you must accept that much."

"That's true. But what's the point of digging up something that happened thirty years ago? People grow up, change, and forget about each other. Otherwise, life would be impossible, don't you think?"

I was on the brink of tears, something that hadn't happened to me since I was a teenager. I decided to put an end to the meeting before I embarrassed myself any further, but Gabriela delivered one last blow.

"You must be very lonely if you feel the need to rummage around in such a distant past."

While I signaled to the waiter to bring the bill, I tried to find the perfect riposte and put an end to the matter in a more or less dignified way. Nothing came to me.

Gabriela looked at me with concern, as if she suddenly felt responsible for my pain, but I had just experienced her contempt and wasn't willing to face her pity as well. I stood up and, leaving her still sitting at the table, said, "I'm sorry for bothering you."

As I walked away I felt as if I'd aged thirty years.

Buddha's Consolation

The wound was so deep I had to go somewhere to lick it in order not to bleed to death. I got home convinced I'd burned all my boats. The gondoliers would have to sing their songs somewhere else, for I had no wish to hear them again.

With a newly hardened heart I rushed up to Titus's apartment to immerse myself in the chapter that was entirely appropriate to my situation: "Treasures of Solitude."

On Titus's bookshelves I found two American books on the matter and thought they'd contain a few clues: *Party of One: The Loner's Manifesto* and *Celebrating Time Alone: Stories of Splendid Solitude*. It's incredible how books like these can make a virtue or obligation out of necessity.

The former referred to some well-known loners like Newton or Michelangelo, who "were never part of the choir" and were fine with that. The latter was more concerned with the specific benefits of solitude. I made a few notes to refer to when I was writing the chapter:

> Living alone is the new millennium's predominant lifestyle.
> It favors one's own priorities and decision making.

171

It offers a maximum degree of freedom.

It puts time at our own disposal.

It helps us to find meaning in our own lives.

It brings us closer to self-knowledge and godliness.

I had to leave it at that as I was getting depressed. I could see now that accepting maxims like this was akin to burying myself alive, just when—in spite of everything else—I'd stuck my head out into the world. I'd blown my chance of being with Gabriela, but I wasn't yet ready to don the hermit's robes.

There's a whole world out there, even if I don't always understand it.

Comforted by this thought, I made dinner, gave Mishima some cat food and fresh water, and did the dishes as I listened to the radio. Yes, I was probably something of a hermit, but I was prepared to come down from the mountain.

I decided that, however much it hurt, I'd banish any hopes I had about Gabriela and embark on a new path, no matter where it would take me. I'd let those who are tired of living enjoy the treasures of solitude. I needed to get started.

I got into bed and started reading Buddha's soothing words. One page, chosen at random, comforted me in my despair before I dropped off to sleep.

Let us be thankful, for if we have not
    learned a lot today,
we have at least learned a little; and if we
    have not learned a little,
we have at least not fallen ill; and if we
    have fallen ill,
we have at least not died, and for this we
    are thankful.

IV

Words to Be Invented

Nocturne

Several days went by and nothing happened. I was waiting for Valdemar's visit, but there was no sign of him. He also failed to turn up at the bar. It was as if he'd vanished into thin air.

I spoke with Titus on the phone a couple of times, and the conversation usually proceeded along predictable lines. He'd say he was recovering slowly but surely; he'd ask about Amalfi's book; I'd exaggerate the amount of work I'd done in order to reassure him. I'd put an abrupt end to our chat before he could ask about Gabriela and promise to call him again.

Titus, however, was a sly old fox and guessed the truth.

"Samuel, I can tell that things aren't going so well for you."

"What are you talking about?" I protested.

"The most important thing is to keep loving life. As Freud said, we must begin to love so as not to fall ill."

It surprised me to hear these words spoken by a seriously ill man. On second thought, perhaps that was precisely what had given him the right perspective.

Titus ended the conversation with words that seemed to come out of the blue, but I took note.

"Good-bye Samuel, and remember that nothing happens without a reason."

Now that I was liberated from my romantic delusions, I could devote all my energy to nourishing my routine. In the literature course, we'd finished with Hesse and moved on to Bertolt Brecht. The February exams were about to start, and a few tears would be shed in my office. Just like every other year.

One Wednesday evening, when I was preparing my class on Brecht, I had a strange premonition. As I was brushing up on a list of his plays, I was struck by the certainty that something was going to change. I can't explain how I came to this conclusion, but the fact is I knew that the routine into which I'd settled was as illusory as it was temporary.

I went to bed with yet another conviction. My rebirth as Francis Amalfi was endangering my mental health. And I'd written only a dozen pages. I had to finish it before I went completely off the rails.

A loud buzzing woke me. Flustered and not yet fully awake, I heard a second buzzing sound which made sure that I was no longer asleep. Somebody was ringing the doorbell at the street level.

I checked the time on my digital alarm clock. It

was just after three in the morning. Feeling terribly tired, I sat up, cursing the drunk who was making such a nuisance of himself after closing time—because only a drunk or a madman could be ringing the doorbell at this hour.

I dragged myself along the hallway on legs that were still asleep, thinking about the curses I was going to rain on the head of the unwanted visitor. There was another possible explanation for this intrusion, which I didn't want to think about. However, when I answered on the intercom my worst fears were confirmed.

"It's Valdemar. I need help."

Hiding Place

Valdemar came up the stairs, visibly terrified. Before explaining what had happened, he dumped a mysterious metal box, a large canvas bag, and the backpack in which he usually carried his manuscript in the hallway.

I ushered him into the living room. I was about to turn on the light, but Valdemar, who'd flopped onto my couch, said, "No, please don't. It's better if we stay in the dark."

He lit a cigarette without asking for permission. It was the first time I'd seen him smoking.

I handed him an ashtray and sat in the chair facing him. In the darkness of the living room I thought about how disconcerting it was to have a conversation with someone whose face is hidden. He hadn't even taken off his hat; I could see its silhouette. He took a deep drag on his cigarette, its glow lighting up his face for a few seconds. Then he said, "Samuel, I'll be straight with you. I have nowhere to go."

That's a great start.

"I'm renting an apartment," he continued. "It's true that I've sometimes been a bit behind with the rent, but the landlady's been quite understanding. After the fire she changed her mind and gave me three days to leave. Today was the last day."

I was alarmed. "What fire?" I asked as he stubbed out his cigarette in the ashtray.

"Someone set fire to my door. I suppose the idea was that the flames would spread inside the apartment. But, don't worry, my manuscript is safe."

"Your manuscript?" Now I was completely flabbergasted. "Do you think someone tried to burn the house down in order to destroy your manuscript?"

"And me with it. There are people who want me out of the way. They know I'm discovering certain things. That's why I asked you not to turn on the light. I don't want them to know that I'm here talking to you. I'm telling you this for your own safety."

I wondered if the whole thing was a figment of his imagination, the paranoid fantasy of a man who believed he could read the future in a chessboard. Yet the fact he'd come to my apartment in the wee hours bringing all his possessions with him was quite unnerving.

"What are you going to do now?" I asked.

"I need to lie low for a while until they forget about me. I don't want to put you in any danger. Let me sleep here tonight and I'll leave tomorrow."

"Are you looking for somewhere to hide?"

"Yes, I am. To hide from myself too. I've taken too many risks lately."

A crazy idea flashed into my mind and remained there, demanding my attention. My place had just one bedroom, so I could only offer Valdemar the couch, with all the inconvenience that would entail. Looking up at the ceiling, I said, "I have the keys to the apartment upstairs. Strictly speaking it's for my use only, but I suppose the owner wouldn't find out if you stayed there for a few days."

"It's unoccupied?" He seemed very interested.

"It belongs to an old editor who's had a bout of angina. He gave me his keys so that I could help him finish a book he'd started to work on. But I can use my own computer for that."

"What kind of book is this?"

"Nothing that would be of any interest to you. It's an anthology of inspirational texts called *A Short Course in Everyday Magic*. As you can see, I have my dark side too."

"We all do." He suddenly brightened up. "And it's our obligation to travel there and explore it. But it's a dangerous journey."

"You're the living proof of that," I said with a yawn.

I was trying to send him a signal to make him understand it was time to sleep, but Valdemar was now in good spirits and it wasn't going to be so easy to make him give up the chance to expound on his visions.

"Before the space race started, the dark side

of the moon led people to imagine the most extraordinary things. That's why the first photos were such a big deal, but also such a disappointment."

"What did they expect to discover on the dark side of the moon?"

"People thought there were moon men who'd gone to hide on the far side because they were afraid we were going to ruin things for them. But the scientists knew perfectly well that there was nothing there."

"So, why so much interest in the photos and going there?"

"That's if they did go there," Valdemar specified. "There are no limits to human curiosity, and sometimes we forget about the risks that come with it. Unless you're prepared to lead a marginal existence, it's better not to know everything, believe me."

"Is that what your book's about?"

"Yes, it's a chronicle of the discoveries that have led me to this point. I began with the mysteries of the moon: the contradictions of the space missions, the real possibilities of settling there, when that might happen, immortality, and so on. The whole lot. But this was just the preliminary work. It took me a while to get to the real truth. The dark side of the moon is a reflection of the human soul. Forget about the space race. That's child's play compared with what's really there."

Afternoon Tea and a Cat

I woke up still feeling tired after our long night-time conversation. Somewhere between the moon and the human soul, Valdemar had gone back to the "platform people" episode.

"Maybe they were the ones who tried to burn down my door. Perhaps they haven't forgiven me for discovering that they hang around there without ever boarding a train."

I'd gotten him to abandon that theory, mainly because I didn't believe that anyone would want to attack this poor man. I told him that there was probably a much simpler explanation: someone, maybe Valdemar himself, had dropped a still-burning cigarette butt next to the door. This had set fire to the doormat, which had created a nasty-smelling smoke.

Valdemar had taken his things up to Titus's apartment, and we'd arranged to meet the next evening. Meanwhile, I had to contend with my own drowsiness and the apathy of my students, most of whom had skipped the class because they'd started to study for exams.

I no longer had a reason to go to the bar, so I used my lunch break to go to the vet. I'd seen on the appointment card Meritxell had given me that

Mishima was due for his second shot, so I asked her when I could bring him in.

"This afternoon I have a home visit very close to where you live. If you want me to come by, it'll save you the trip. I'll charge you as if you'd come to the clinic, OK?"

It was clear that she liked me. The cat was a secondary matter. I could start planning for the hot chocolate with ladyfingers because it was about to become a reality. However, some pretense was necessary, as Meritxell was shy and would never admit she was more interested in going to meet the owner than treating his cat.

"All right," I agreed, "but don't tell me what time you're planning to come—and I'll also try to forget that you're coming, so Mishima won't hide again."

"That's a good tactic," she said and winked before disappearing behind the door of her consulting room.

I went back to the university in order to have a bite to eat before my next class at four. The bar of the philology faculty, a veritable underground rats' nest, is not the most comfortable of places, but I opted for killing time there.

I have a social life. I felt smug as I munched on the second sandwich of the day.

Since Mishima's arrival, a ragtag bunch of acquaintances had entered my life: the old man,

Valdemar, and now Meritxell. It seemed that they all needed something from me. The cat wanted an owner; Titus, a substitute editor; Valdemar, a hiding place for his fears and late-night conver-sation. In Meritxell's case, I imagined she was just looking for a bit of friendship.

There was one exception, but I didn't want to dwell on that. I was delighted to be of use to the others. I could never have imagined this. For the first time I realized that the most important indicator of our value in this world is the good we do unto others.

Unlearning the Learned

Before entering my apartment, I went upstairs to make sure nothing was amiss. I put my ear to the door, but I couldn't detect any sign of activity. Valdemar was probably sleeping. He needed to gather strength in order to keep me awake all night.

Looking forward to my afternoon snack with Meritxell, I forgot that I was supposed to conceal it from myself so that Mishima wouldn't get wind of it. My homecoming, complete with a bag of ladyfingers, didn't go unnoticed and, after some rushing up and down the passage, he vanished. This time I didn't bother to go looking for him.

I put the ladyfingers on the kitchen counter next to the container of cocoa and dropped into my chair without any feeling of regret. I wanted to make the most of the waning afternoon light to leaf through the dictionary of untranslatable words again.

While I flipped through the pages, I came across a familiar term, *dharma*. I read the entry:

What is my place in the universe? What is the best way to live my life? How do I find the right answers to the previous questions? The spiritual traditions of the world have been built upon the human impulse to seek such answers.

Writing Amalfi's book had taught me to skim works like this, so I skipped the etymological history of the term and the outline of Hindu cosmology. I stopped at a reference to one of Kerouac's novels, *The Dharma Bums*, which I'd read years earlier. This Beat Generation classic had inspired the author of the dictionary to reflect:

Finding ways of learning and following one's own dharma doesn't mean blind submission to one god or doctrine. Rather, it means recognition of the fact that the right way of living can lead to the enlightenment of all those beings who feel it, a declaration that each and every person has a unique chance to discover the essential truth.

My reading was cut short by the doorbell and the arrival of Meritxell. When she reached the landing and rang at the door of my apartment, I was leaning against the wall waiting for her. She came in with a small bag, in a disconcertingly good mood. I noticed that she was wearing eyeliner and that she'd used some kind of gel to give her short hair a tousled look. Girls who are naturally beautiful should be forbidden from using such unnecessary embellishments.

"I've got two bits of news, one good and the other bad. Which one do you want to hear first?" I asked.

She laughed. "The bad news. You should always start with the bad news."

"I can't find the cat. He's run off to hide somewhere again."

"Well, that's not the end of the world. So what's the good news, then?"

"I can make you hot chocolate with lady-fingers."

"I never have chocolate in any form. I'm allergic to it. But I'll come in and rest for a moment. I'm completely done in!"

She sat down on the couch, and I went to heat the milk for the hot chocolate and get her an orange juice, surreptitiously keeping an eye on what the lovely vet was up to. She checked her hair a couple of times and then inspected everything I had in my living room. She seemed to feel at home, while at the same time she had an expectant look on her face, although I wasn't sure what she was hoping for.

I served our afternoon snack and drew my chair closer to the table. I could have sat next to her on the couch—there was plenty of room for both of us—but that was a risky option. If I was wrong and Meritxell didn't want anything from me, she'd feel uncomfortable with my nearness. If, on the contrary, she was foolish enough to want something from me, then she'd expect me to put my arm around her at some point in the conversation. After that, anything could happen.

Solution: I sat across from her to see what would happen. I simply wanted to have an afternoon snack in good company without any further expectations.

"I live alone too," she offered. "I shared a place for years, but then all of a sudden I needed to have my own space."

"I've always had the same feeling," I confessed, "although, since the new year, things have been getting complicated. Not that I wanted any of it."

"What do you mean?"

I was on the verge of telling her what love in lowercase had done to my life, but I changed my mind just in time, because I didn't want to bore her.

"Let's say that my solitude is very noisy, like that novel by Hrabal."

"Who's Hrabal?"

"A Czech writer. Sorry, we teachers have the bad habit of lacing our conversation with literary references, which is a pretty stupid thing to do."

"Why is it stupid? It's always good to learn something new."

"Up to a point it is, but knowing too much can

be very awkward. Valdemar's a good example of that."

"Who's Valdemar?"

"It's better not to know."

"So according to you, nobody should know anything!"

"OK, Buddha once said that knowledge should be like a boat. You can use it to get across the river, but once you reach the other side it's absurd to keep lugging it with you. Do you know what I mean?"

"You've used Buddha's words to explain yourself."

"You see? I'm hopeless. That's what I mean. I have to unlearn everything I've learned and go back to being a normal person. Culture is just background noise that prevents me from seeing life as it really is. Culture makes no one happy. I want to be a simpleton or a wise peasant who knows when it's going to rain and goes to bed and wakes up when the sun sets and rises.

"My brother has a farm near Berga," she said teasingly. "He might lend you a hoe if you ask him nicely."

"What I need is a good whack on the head."

The phone started to ring, interrupting the unexpectedly animated conversation. I didn't have a clue why I was saying all of this, but my guest seemed to be enjoying herself, so I declared, "I'm not going to get it. I'm never going to answer the phone again. We're on strike against background noise that won't let us see life as it really is."

At the third ring the answering machine came on. The message made me spill hot chocolate on my sweater.

"Samuel, I'm sorry about what happened last week. I think I was being unfair. Can you forgive me? There are lots of things you don't know about me. Actually, you know nothing. Or almost nothing."

The contralto voice seemed to quaver with the last few words, and the message ended.

My heart had clenched like a fist, but I made a huge effort to forget about what I'd just heard and continue the conversation. Meritxell no longer looked relaxed on my couch. She seemed uncom-fortable at having heard these intimate words that had also relegated her to second fiddle. No woman was going to put up with that.

I mumbled, not very convincingly, "See what I mean? You can't live in peace these days."

The phone rang again, destroying any remnant of coziness between us. I didn't dare to speak and, even less, to take the call. I was a plucked chicken, cowering in my chair.

It was Gabriela again, completing her previous message.

"What I was trying to say was that I'd like to see you again if you're not angry with me.

Perhaps we can be friends. I promise to behave. My phone number is—"

Even before she had finished speaking, Meritxell stood up and got her bag and coat, saying, "It's getting late."

I walked her to the door in a state of utter confusion. Before I could think of a suitable way of saying good-bye, she added, "You're right. Your solitude is very noisy. Good-bye."

Leitmotif

Valdemar didn't turn up that night as arranged, but I didn't make the effort to go to see him either.

Once in bed, I began to review everything that had happened that surprising day. I came to what I thought was an interesting conclusion: every day has a certain tone or leitmotif. By the end of the afternoon I'd already understood what the leitmotif of that day had been: "They want to be with you."

When you're feeling lonely this might appear to be a blessing, but the bottom line is that it can be complicated if you're not ready for it. In order to accept the love of others, you need a wise heart because rejection's easier to cope with than love. You can turn against someone who is attacking you, but what are you supposed to do when someone reveals their love for you?

Before I went to sleep I thought that it was very nice of Meritxell to want to have an afternoon snack with me and put up with my blathering. Despite her abrupt departure, there had been something between us that enabled us to reveal ourselves as we were, without being afraid of saying or doing something wrong.

But, what about Gabriela? Why had she called me just then?

It was as if, from a distance, she'd noticed that I was starting to get involved with someone else, and she wanted to put a stop to it so that my yearnings would again be focused on her. But why?

Fear of being loved was the reason behind my long period of solitude, and it might also explain Gabriela's vehemence when she rejected me on our first meeting.

Lesson number 1: whatever they say, life is never easy.

Those Who Know Should Enlighten Those Who Don't

I'd worked hard on my introductory class on Bertolt Brecht. The students aren't huge fans of his, perhaps because we live in times that are too cynical for ethical considerations. And he is essentially a moral writer.

What I like most about Brecht are the titles he gives his plays—for example, *The Caucasian Chalk Circle* or *The Good Person of Szechwan*. Rather than boring my students with Brecht's biography, I discussed this latter work, which is a very good example of his more didactic phase.

The play opens with a discussion between three gods as to whether a good and just character can survive in a world of selfish people. They decide to put their theories to the test with Shen Teh, a prostitute who lives in Szechwan, and the only person who is willing to offer the hospitality of her cottage to three strangers who have come to her town. Thinking about her neighbors and their needs, she uses the money the strangers give her to open a shop, but people are so ruthless in taking advantage of her goodness that she goes out of business.

Having learned her lesson, she starts again, this time disguised as a tough man whom all the customers respect, although they wistfully wonder what has become of the kindhearted Shen Teh. In the end she reveals herself, and they're all amazed at her stratagem.

The underlying question is: in order to be good, should one adopt the guise of a bad person?

I'd told them this much when a student raised his hand. It was the first time I'd seen him in my class that term. I was expecting him to open the discussion about goodness, fear, and all the rest, but his question was much more banal.

"Does Szechwan exist?"

The few students who'd turned up for the class sniggered at the naïveté of the question.

"Yes, I think it's called Sichuan these days. I know that because they have some giant-panda sanctuaries there. I saw a documentary about them."

They all started laughing.

What's so funny about that? I had to go on the offensive in order to regain my dignity as a teacher.

"It makes no difference whether the story takes place in Szechwan or Samarkand. Bertolt Brecht used an exotic setting to produce a parable about goodness. I suppose you know what a parable is, or am I mistaken?"

The smart girl with the round glasses went into action. "It's a story with a message, like the ones in the New Testament."

"Exactly. Contemporary writers also use the device. Adorno, the German Marxist philosopher, said that Kafka's fiction works, especially *The Castle*, are primarily parables. But *The Good Person of Szechwan* isn't a sententious work like the New Testament stories, and neither does it hold out a pessimistic view of things as Kafka does. It's an invitation to reflect on a fairly complicated matter. In this regard it's more like the Nasreddin stories. Does anyone know who Nasreddin is?"

Round-Specs offered, "I think it's a Sufi thing."

"Very good. Nasreddin is the main character of many Sufi exemplary tales. There's one about wisdom that I think is especially good. Would you like to hear it?"

Not a peep out of anyone, which was perfectly in keeping with this Middle Eastern story. I therefore began:

"Nasreddin came to a small village where they mistook him for a famous wise man. He didn't want to disappoint the people who'd gathered in the square, so he opened up his arms and said, 'I imagine that, since you're here, you know what I'm going to tell you.'

"The people said, 'No, what do you have to tell us? We don't know. Tell us, please.'

"Nasreddin replied, 'If you've come here without knowing what I want to say, then you're not ready to hear it.'

"Then he stood up and walked away. The crowd was shocked by his abrupt departure. They were about to write him off as a madman when some-one said, 'How clever he is! He's totally right. How could we dare to come here without knowing what we were coming to hear? How stupid we've been. Now we've wasted a wonderful opportunity. How brilliant he is! How wise he is! Let us ask this man to come and speak to us a second time.'

"Some of the villagers went to find him and begged him to come back, saying that his knowledge was too vast for a single lecture. After all their pleading, Nasreddin went back to the same square. Now the crowd was twice its previous size. Once again he said, 'I imagine that you know what I'm going to tell you.'

"Having learned their lesson, the people nodded and someone spoke up. 'Of course we know. That is why we have come.'

"On hearing this, Nasreddin looked down and said, 'Well, since you know what I have to say to you, there is no need to repeat it.'

"He left the square and walked away. The people were dumbfounded. Then one fanatic started to shout, 'Brilliant! Marvelous! We want him to give us more of his wisdom!'

"A delegation of village notables went to find him and begged him on their knees to come back and give a third and final lecture. They beseeched him so persistently that he agreed to come back for the last time. When he reached the square he was greeted by roars of a veritable multitude. Once again, he said, 'I imagine that you know what I'm going to tell you.'

"This time the people had come to an agreement and had nominated the head man of the village to speak for them. The head man said, 'Some do and some don't.'

"The crowd fell silent and everyone looked at Nasreddin, who concluded, 'Then those who know should enlighten those who don't.'

"Having said that, he left."

Heaven

The tale of Nasreddin brought the class to a successful conclusion. As those stories have been around for hundreds of years, there's something to be said for the oral tradition.

I had another class early that afternoon, so I decided to go for a walk and make the most of the sun. I crossed the Plaça de la Universitat and dived into the Raval quarter. After walking past a Russian bookshop, I went down Carrer de les Egipcíaques.

This is one of the few streets I go down simply because I like the name. Since my midday meetings with Valdemar had come to an end, I was a little lost, and I started roaming around, up one street and down the next, without stopping anywhere.

After an hour of this aimless meandering around the neighborhood, I sat down under a palm tree on the Rambla del Raval.

You're such a moron, wandering around like this because you can't decide whether to call her or not.

I looked at my watch and saw that it was half past two. Gabriela was probably on her way home, or walking through the streets like I was.

She'd given me her cell phone number, so there would be no problem finding her.

I dug a couple of coins out of my pockets and unfolded the bit of paper on which I'd written her number. I must have been learning the hard way, because I didn't feel too nervous as I waited for her to answer.

"Hello?"

That changed everything: just hearing that question was enough to rekindle the flame. But I'd promised myself I'd handle myself with dignity.

"Hi, this is Samuel."

"Hello, Samuel. Where are you?"

"Everywhere and nowhere. I'm working at what they call killing time."

"Not a bad job," she said in the affable tone of someone speaking to a small child. "Do you do that often?"

"I try to."

"I was in bed, about to have a nap."

"I'm running out of money and don't have any more coins. Tell me when and where to meet."

The silence barely lasted an instant. "Tomorrow, six o'clock, at Caelum."

"I don't know where that is. What did you say it's called?"

"Just think about heaven."

We were cut off. Though I didn't know where we were supposed to meet, I felt very calm. I leaned against a palm tree and did as I was told.

I stared at the sky and, all at once, the world seemed to make sense again. The children's shouts weren't noise but life in the purest state; the wind wasn't a chilling knife thrust but a cool caress.

I looked again at the scrap of paper. I liked seeing her name written next to the nine numbers. *Gabriela*.

None of This Is Real

"You know what? I often have the feeling that my accident in Patagonia didn't end the way I think it did."

Valdemar was on the couch, smoking in the darkness again. He'd come downstairs just before midnight, when I was about to go to bed. It seemed that he was at his most lucid at midday and late at night.

"Really? So how did it end?"

Valdemar's sweaty forehead momentarily glistened in the faint light of a deep drag on his cigarette. "Sometimes I imagine that I died in that accident. You're right. It's impossible to survive a fall of one hundred feet. Ever since then, everything that's happened has been only a dream—the path on the bank of the frozen river, the flash of my camera, being rescued, the hospital, my return to Barcelona, this conversation, and all the rest—none of it's real."

"If it's not real, how come we're sitting here talking about it now?"

"It's part of a dream, the only place where the dead can live."

"So I'm part of your dream?"

"More or less."

"That means I don't have a life of my own. I

exist just in your head or, worse, in the eternal dream of a dead man."

"Something like that."

We drifted into a long minute of silence. Valdemar, hatless this time, was blowing clouds of smoke toward the ceiling, in shapes I couldn't make out. Then he seemed troubled by some thought and sat upright, crushing the butt in the ashtray.

"When are you going to stop fretting and embrace nothingness at last?" He was going for the jugular.

"Maybe when I'm sure I'm dead."

"That's the biggest joke of all, because there's no way we'll ever know that."

Date in Heaven

I had to do a bit of research in order to discover where I'd arranged to meet Gabriela at six that afternoon. Her comment, "Think about heaven," confirmed that the name of the place was Caelum—Latin for "sky."

During my lunch break I went to the Fnac bookshop to check out the Barcelona city guides and eventually found Caelum in a list of "charming" cafés and restaurants. It was in one of the backstreets near Plaça del Pi, and I learned that it was a tearoom that served only cakes and biscuits made by nuns.

Somewhat surprised by this choice, I jotted down the address in my diary and went home to have a nap.

My alarm went off at five, and Mishima started circling around my bed. I had the impression I'd slept for only a few seconds, but the clock clearly showed that my nap had lasted an hour and a half. Too long.

I got out of bed and staggered into the shower, where the hot water gradually woke me up. I was wondering whether I should shave or not. Most women like clean-shaven men, especially if they have to kiss their cheeks by way of greeting. Then again, if I looked too dapper, I'd be admitting that the date was very important for me. And that might put her on the defensive.

So in the end I decided not to shave, though I did put on the best clothes in my humble wardrobe: some gray trousers, which were quite stylish, and a somewhat tight blue sweater. My long overcoat provided the requisite bohemian touch.

Let's go. I locked my door believing that when I came back I'd be a new man.

Where God Looks

To my surprise, Gabriela was already there when I arrived at the agreed time. Before going inside I saw her, looking like a mirage in the tearoom window. The place was lit only by the tremulous glimmering of candles, creating an atmosphere that was somewhere between monastic and romantic.

Gabriela was studying the list of teas when I nervously presented myself at her table.

Should I greet her in the usual way with a kiss on each cheek? I opted to sit down and see what happened. I greeted her shyly and started perusing the menu. Since I don't know much about tea, I ordered a Lady Grey, simply because the name appealed to me.

"I'll have the same, please," Gabriela said to the waitress, who asked if we'd like some of the nuns' cakes as well.

"Not yet, thank you," I answered for both of us, still surprised that she'd asked for the same as me.

After these formalities, we sat there looking at one another in silence. I saw that she wasn't wearing earrings, but she did have two butterfly clips holding back her wavy hair. In my addled state, I interpreted this as a good omen.

While I was trying to think of some way of starting up a conversation, Gabriela, who'd been turning her empty cup round and round in her hands, said without looking at me, "Japanese craftsmen are geniuses when they make cups. Do you know which part requires the most effort?"

"I don't know. The handle maybe?"

"Japanese cups don't have handles."

"How do you know?"

"I lived there long enough to find out."

"You lived in Japan?"

"You haven't answered my question." She frowned teasingly.

"I suppose they make an effort to keep the decoration on the outside of the cup as simple and harmonious as possible. Something very Zen."

"No, not that."

"Then they try hard to make it perfectly round."

"No. An irregularly shaped cup can be a work of art."

"I give up. Which part is it then?"

"The bottom of the cup, the part you can't see—and do you know why?"

"No idea."

"That's where God looks."

"They must have a word for that," I replied, as the waitress served our tea.

"What do you mean?"

"The Japanese must have a word for the hidden beauty that only God can see. If not, they should invent one."

"How do you know? Have you lived in Japan?" She laughed, then blew on her hot tea.

"No, but I've got a dictionary of strange words. Lots of them exist only in Japanese, and I get the impression that they live in a separate world with codes that only they can understand."

"It's a bit like that."

A sad expression crossed her face, and she used her index finger to block a tear that was trying to escape.

It was evident that I'd accidentally tugged at something that she didn't want touched. This was confirmed by the swiftness of her next comment, so that I wouldn't have time to ask any further questions: "This dictionary sounds appealing. But I'd be even more interested in one made up of words that don't exist and need to be invented, as you just said. I'm sure you could do that."

"What makes you think I could write a dictionary?"

"You look like someone who'd do that kind of thing."

I was annoyed by her comment, mostly because it was true. Only someone like me would set out to do that kind of thing. Francis Amalfi's book— even if I was doing it as a favor to Titus—was a similar type of project. I went on the offensive.

"You've persuaded me. I think I'll write one. But I'll need your help. What other concepts need a name, apart from the beauty that only God sees?"

"There are lots of words that need to be invented. Why do we have the term 'orphan' for a child who loses his or her mother when there's none for a mother who loses her child? Does she suffer less, perhaps?"

"You're right. Now that I'm thinking about it, I have a definition that requires a word for it: love in lowercase."

"Love in lowercase?"

"It's when some small act of kindness sets off a chain of events that comes around again in the form of multiplied love. Then, even if you want to return to where you started, it's too late, because this love in lowercase has wiped away all traces of the path back to where you were before."

"That sounds beautiful, but I'm not sure I understand."

"I don't understand it myself. But the proof that it exists is that we're here."

I immediately regretted having revealed myself. It had all gone well so far and, like an idiot, I'd messed it up at the last moment.

She confirmed my fears. "It's getting late. I must get home."

We both stood up. "Where do you live?" I asked.

"In Plaça dels Àngels."

"Let me walk with you some of the way," I offered spontaneously.

"No, don't bother. I want to think of some words that need inventing."

What an excuse! But Gabriela had fallen into her own trap.

"If I'm going to write this dictionary, I'll need to know what entries you come up with. Can I take you to lunch one day? There's a restaurant in Gràcia, and I've never been able to work out why it's called what it is. It's the perfect place for inventing words."

"What's the name?" Gabriela was already on the street, buttoning up her coat.

"Buzzing. When would you like to go?"

She gave me an exasperated look. She could see that I wasn't going to let her go without her granting me another date, so she said, "Thursday perhaps."

"That works for me. Since you don't know where it is, I'll come to the shop and we can go there together."

"As you wish."

I kissed her on both cheeks to say good-bye.

"You're prickly," she said with a faint smile, and walked away. This made me think that not all was lost.

A Spark in the Darkness

In the Metro, on my way to the hospital, I felt totally embarrassed about what I'd done. The fact that I was in love with Gabriela didn't give me the right to pressure her the way I had when we said good-bye.

It was lovely to have tea with you, Gabriela. If you like, we can do it again some afternoon. You know where to find me. That would have been the most elegant and sensitive thing to say.

If I'd said that, she probably wouldn't have felt under duress and might have called me again. But no, I'd forced her to agree to another date. Now, in all likelihood, she'd phone before Thursday and leave me a message to cancel it. My just deserts.

Making my way along the endless corridors of the hospital, I realized it was almost a month since I'd last been to visit Titus. That wasn't good. Yes, we'd talked on the phone a couple of times a week, but that wasn't enough. After all, thanks to a section of model-train track, Titus had enabled me to step down from the train heading toward a life of solitude.

He seemed a lot more frail to me this time,

probably because I hadn't seen him for so long. His small bald head was nestled so deep in the pillow that it looked as if it was about to disappear.

I sat down beside him as a porter wheeled off his roommate, a man of about fifty with a dreadful cough.

I got to the point right away. "I've let you down."

I feel guilty: the leitmotif of the day.

"Enough of that! I don't think I have much longer to live, so listen carefully. I have something important to tell you."

With a feeling of dread, I moved my chair closer. His voice was so weak it was difficult to understand him.

"This is purgatory, Samuel. But you can learn important lessons in purgatory."

I tried to distract him from this gloomy talk by bringing up the only thing I thought might console him.

"Sorry to change the subject, but do you remember the mad physicist I told you about?"

"Valdemar."

"Good memory. Well, the other day he said that his life's just a dream and that, in reality, he's dead. Maybe he's right and we're all dead. Or real life is just what we see and do when we dream. What I'm trying to say is . . . well, he said that none of this is real, so we shouldn't worry. And you shouldn't worry either, even if you are having a bad time right now."

Titus rubbed his hand over his unshaven chin, as if looking for the right words. He seemed calm enough. Then he cleared his throat and said very slowly, "This damn Valdemar is right. We can't be sure that this is the only world in existence. Call it a dream or an illusion or whatever you like. But we're just a spark of consciousness in the darkness of the universe. But since the time that comes before us and that which comes afterward are infinite, we might say that this spark never happened. Are you with me?"

"More or less. But what is this important thing you want to tell me?"

"I'm telling you now, damn it!"

After raising his voice, Titus was gasping, so short of breath I was on the verge of ringing for a nurse. But he grabbed my arm to stop me. After a few ragged attempts at trying to breathe steadily again, he got some color back in his face.

"Don't push yourself," I whispered. "There's no need. If you want to talk, take it slowly. I've got all the time in the world."

"But I haven't. Please don't interrupt me."

I nodded and clasped my hands like a good boy. When he began to speak, I could see that he'd been rehearsing the words for some time. They were his farewell to me.

"We live too far away from the outer galaxies.

We'll never be able to reach them. We're also too far away from the quantum universe, so we can't understand it. We'll never get across the last threshold of matter. If we did, we'd discover that nothing exists, as Valdemar says. We live in a world of sensations and feelings. Always remember that, Samuel. Never reject your sensations and feelings. They're all you've got."

His words made quite an impression on me. Then Nasreddin's dictum came to mind. *Those who know should enlighten those who don't.* However, I was sure that I'd never have anyone to whom I could confide what Titus had just revealed.

"Now go and don't come back," he added.

I was shocked. "Why?"

Everything I'd felt part of was moving away from me, like an expanding galaxy.

"I have nothing more to say to you. I don't want you to call me either. Leave me alone to play the last round with Death. I fear the cards are stacked against me."

The Price of the Moon

I was devastated when I got home.

When I walked into the living room I was relieved to see that the answering machine wasn't flashing. Gabriela hadn't canceled our date yet, but she probably would sometime before Thursday. Was I getting paranoid?

I put some water on to boil for my pasta and played with Mishima, hoping all the while that Valdemar wouldn't come down to visit. I wasn't in the mood to listen to him. I just wanted to have some dinner and crawl into bed and put an end to the day.

I'd lost Titus, who more than anyone else had been like a father to me. Apart from his final message, which would take me some time to digest, his sad situation had at least given me some perspective on my own. However much I was suffering over Gabriela, it was nothing compared with the distress of a man who was slowly dying in the hospital.

Was that what he was trying to tell me? That I should cling to sensations and feelings as long as I was in the world? It's possible, but Titus's farewell had been too much of a blow for me to be able to act on his advice.

I mixed the spaghetti with some cold tomato

sauce and began to eat it in front of the television, something I don't do often. Oddly enough, they were showing a documentary about the space race.

The film offered a summary of the successes and obstacles faced by more than fifty spaceships that visited the moon, although only twelve men actually managed to walk on it. After *Apollo 17*, which landed on the moon and returned to Earth in December 1972, no one else has been back there, which would seem to bear out Valdemar's suspicions. The next attempt, the Lunar Prospector mission, was carried out with a crewless spacecraft, and it was launched only in 1998.

The episode in question focused on moon dust, the horrible regolith that Valdemar had told me about. It seems that the astronauts who visited the moon brought back some rocks and regolith as souvenirs, which NASA keeps in Houston at 92 degrees below zero.

The strange thing is that, in 2003, three interns at the Johnson Space Center lab were tried for the theft of 101.5 grams of lunar rock samples, which they'd attempted to sell at prices ranging from $1,000 to $5,000 a gram. However, the jury valued the samples at a much higher price, basing its calculations on the fact that each gram had cost the U.S. Treasury $50,800. And since then, the price of moon samples sold to the public has reached even more astronomical levels.

I turned off the TV wondering what sort of idiot would pay that kind of money for a few grains of dust.

Absences

On Wednesday, after having to supervise several exams, I went to the vet. I hadn't seen Meritxell since the afternoon snack that had ended so badly. Despite everything, she greeted me quite warmly.

"I can't leave now. I'm on call till five."

"If you want to come by for an afternoon snack, I'll be at home. Mishima still needs to have his shot, but you know what he's like."

"I'll come prepared, just in case."

I understood that she'd forgiven me and accepted my invitation.

Although a benevolent sun was announcing the advent of spring, I felt too sad to wander around the city. Now I needed the warmth of a friend and, better still, a friend like Meritxell.

Danger was lurking on the horizon of our afternoon snack, which was twenty-four hours before my hypothetical date with Gabriela. This would be an ideal time for her to call with an excuse to cancel it. If we were in the living room and the answering machine started blabbing again, I could say bye-bye to my friendship with Meritxell.

The solution was simple. I'd disconnect the answering machine and even the phone as well.

In fact, I didn't want to know in advance whether Gabriela would be having lunch with me or not. I'd go to collect her as planned, and if she didn't want to join me, I'd eat by myself in the restaurant anyway. There was no point in fretting about it.

Cut off from the outside world except for the doorbell, I devoted the early hours of the afternoon to marking the exam papers for my language and history of literature classes. To my surprise, there were no half measures. Either they were impeccable—revealing that some of my students had at least one German parent—or it took a lot of compassion and practical-mindedness to pass them.

As I impassively worked my way through the exam papers, I wondered what Valdemar was doing all day in the upstairs apartment. The fact of his not coming to bother me didn't mean that the problem didn't exist. How long could I hide him? When Titus died—which might happen at any moment—his family would come and decide what to do with his things. I'd have a right old mess on my hands if they found him there.

My irresponsibility in handling the matter of Valdemar presented an even thornier problem: Francis Amalfi's book. It was ages—or so it seemed to me—since Titus had asked me to take on the job. I should have finished it by now, yet he hadn't given me any details or even the name of the publisher.

The doorbell put an end to my musings. I put the coffeepot on the stove as I listened to Meritxell coming up the stairs.

I welcomed her with a tentative hug and helped her out of her coat. She seemed to be in a good mood once again, which supported my theory that she liked me, not that I'd done anything to deserve that.

She accepted a cup of coffee and half a croissant.

"I can't see Mishima." This was slightly mocking.

"I guess he's gone off to hide again. I think he can detect you from miles away. That's not so surprising. I used to hide under the bed when the doctor came to give me an injection."

I'd just put the cups of coffee and the halved croissant on the table when the doorbell rang twice. That set off alarm bells within me.

"Were you expecting someone else?" Meritxell asked warily.

"Certainly not," I said, heading for the door to see who it was.

The act of opening the door confirmed what I expected to find: Valdemar, hat and all. In these circumstances, a disagreeable sight. Before I had a chance to ask him in—or prevent him from entering—he immediately marched in, heading for the living room.

Following in his wake, I could see that Meritxell

almost jumped out of her skin when she saw him. Valdemar sat down beside her without as much as saying hello.

"He lives upstairs," I informed her, as if that explained anything. "We often have late-night chats, but he's come early today."

"They've found Temis!" He was euphoric and seemed to assume that I, Meritxell, and the rest of humanity should know what he was talking about.

He took off his hat so he could rest his head more comfortably on the back of the couch. "Temístocles García. Temis to his friends. He disappeared on July 5th last year, in the Valle de la Luna."

I went to get an ashtray, trying to avoid further complications. Valdemar was highly excited and very twitchy, and Meritxell was frozen to the spot with a cup of coffee in one hand and half a croissant in the other.

I should take a photo. This looks very much like our last afternoon snack.

"I'm talking about the north of Chile, the Atacama Desert. That's where the Valle de la Luna is, and that's where Temis disappeared. It was a grand mal absence."

"What on earth are you talking about?" I was annoyed with him for ruining our little party.

"I'm no expert in medicine," he said, ignoring my reaction. "But I know there's a sort of epilepsy that causes something called absence seizures. These are divided into two types: petit mal and grand mal. Temístocles had the latter, which is more acute. The afflicted person panics for several hours and can think only about fleeing. If he has money, like my friend had, he'll rush to the airport and get a ticket to the most faraway place possible. When he arrives, he gets a room in a hotel and goes to sleep. The absence attack disappears while he's sleeping, but it also wipes out the memories of everything that happened while it lasted. It's happened to Temis dozens of times. Thanks to some money he inherited, he's woken up in cities all over the world over the past few years. That might sound like fun, but I can assure you it causes great anxiety to people who suffer from this. After his last grand mal seizure, no one knew where he was. But I just phoned a friend in Chile, and he told me they've found him. To be precise, Temístocles has managed to find himself, and now he's ready and waiting for his next absence."

"I have to go," Meritxell said.

Valdemar must have seen her for the first time. He paused and then said, "If you wake up in a strange city, phone us and we'll come and find you. You never know when your first grand mal seizure's going to strike."

What Happened to the Pig?

If she didn't cancel at the last minute, this was going to be my third date with Gabriela. And we were still complete strangers to each other.

All I knew was that she worked in a record shop, that she'd lived in Japan, had gone to ballet classes at some point, and that, when she was taking piano lessons, she'd gotten stuck on the piece called "Spinning Song." It wasn't much to go by.

As for me, she knew only that I liked classical music and that I remembered a children's game from thirty years ago. She also knew I was crazy about her.

I went to the record shop determined to behave like a gentleman no matter what. I was surprised to find Gabriela waiting for me on the street, ready to go. She was wearing a purple coat and a hair band of the same color.

"My colleague's closing up today. We can leave now." She sounded happy.

This saying that women never cease to amaze is not a myth. I was pondering this as we walked up the last bit of La Rambla toward the Plaça de Catalunya.

"Shall we take the Metro?" I asked.

"Let's walk. It's a lovely day."

I looked around. The square was full of tourists basking in the sun and groups of office workers smoking and cracking jokes. Yes, it really was a beautiful day, and all the more so for me, as I was walking through the streets with Gabriela by my side.

A bunch of Japanese tourists clustered around a map prompted me to ask Gabriela, "What kind of work were you doing in Japan?"

I'd chosen my words very carefully. It was much more tactful than asking why she'd gone to live there, or why she'd come back.

"I was teaching English, giving private lessons."

"That's odd. I would've thought the Japanese would want a native speaker. You must speak it very well."

"Not really! I only ever got as far as the Cambridge First Certificate. To tell the truth, hardly anyone speaks English in Japan. It's worse than here. That's why they desperately need teachers, and they pay very well."

"But living there must be very expensive. I imagine you had to give a lot of classes."

"Not so many, actually. I was in Osaka, and in those days I rarely went out. When I wasn't teaching, I was in my room, reading. I'd get through three or four books a week."

What's the point of being in Japan if you lock yourself up in your room?

"Can you read Japanese?"

"No. I can speak it. That's not so difficult. But reading kanji is another matter. It takes years to learn the characters."

"What language were you reading in, then?"

"Mainly English. Osaka is the cultural capital of Japan, or at least that's what they say there. Not far from where I was living there was an American secondhand bookshop. A lot of foreigners used to go there. I'd spend my money on anthologies of short stories. I love stories!"

"You're certainly full of surprises. Who are your favorite writers?"

"A lot of them are quite old-fashioned—for example, Somerset Maugham. But my favorite story is one by Graham Greene called 'A Shocking Accident.' I read it in an anthology. It was the only book I brought back with me when I left Osaka. You won't find it anywhere now. Shall I tell you what it's about?"

I nodded and started walking more slowly. I felt so privileged having her there at my side that I wished the Passeig de Gràcia would go on forever.

Gabriela began to tell the story.

"The main character is Jerome, the son of a struggling writer who travels a lot. Since the writer is a widower, he sends the boy to a boarding school in England while he's away, working in Italy. The boy worships his father and imagines him as a secret agent and many other things. One day, the housemaster calls him to his room to break the news that his father has died, taking care to add that he didn't suffer. Naturally, Jerome wants to know what happened. The housemaster is reluctant to discuss the details but, as the boy insists, tells him that it was a very strange accident. As he was walking along a street in Naples, his father passed beneath a balcony on which somebody was keeping a pig. The pig was overfed and very fat, and when his father was directly underneath the balcony, it broke and the pig fell on him, killing him instantly.

"When Jerome asks, 'What happened to the pig?' the housemaster interprets this as callousness and sends him back to his room.

"Jerome grows up to be a lonely, rather melancholy man. He accepts that his father wasn't a spy but refuses to tell people how he died, because on the few occasions he has done so they have laughed at him. The secret becomes a millstone around his neck. One day he meets a girl and starts going out with her. He conceals the story of his father's death from her because he knows that if she laughs, he will never be able to marry her. But when they go to visit his aunt one day, the girl sees a photo of his father and asks about it. The aunt spills the beans. Jerome's fiancée merely says, 'It makes you think, doesn't it. Happening like that. Out of a clear sky.'

"On the way home, Jerome asks her what she's thinking.

" 'I was wondering,' she says, 'what happened to the poor pig.'

"That's when Jerome realizes he's found the love of his life."

Put It on My Karma Account

The owner of the restaurant told us that they had chosen the name "Buzzing" as an omen of success, as the word is often used to describe a place full of people having a great time.

His fringe was dyed in psychedelic colors to go with the black, red, and orange decor and the sixties-inspired furniture. Gabriela stood for a moment contemplating a series of black-and-white photos covering one of the walls. Then she asked, "Have you got any new entries for the dictionary?"

"A couple of things." I was trying to improvise because I hadn't really come up with anything. "It's a variation on love in lowercase, the instant karma that happens when you commit minor indiscretions. You complain that a friend is stingy, and that day he gives you a gift. Or you shout at someone, and when you go outside you're so agitated you crash into a lamppost. The Germans have a saying for this, which roughly translated is 'God punishes small sins without delay.'"

"That's quite good."

The man with the multicolored fringe poured our wine while we decided on what to eat. I raised my glass to make a toast with Gabriela. *Here's to us.* But I resisted the temptation to say anything, because that would have sounded too cheesy, so we clinked our glasses in silence.

"When can I see you again?" I asked, breaking my own rule about not pressuring her.

She ignored my question. "I've got a new entry for your dictionary. The definition would be: the inability of some people to live in the present."

"That's not fair," I protested.

Gabriela smiled and, after taking a sip of her wine, said, "Put it on my karma account."

10,000 Ways to Say
I Love You

Anyone who's in love wants to get to know his beloved's past. This is one of the ways to understand and avoid disappointing her. In my case, Gabriela's past was still quite a mystery, but knowing she'd lived in Osaka and spoke Japanese made me decide, that very afternoon, to enroll in an intensive course on Japanese culture.

I didn't have many resources on the subject at home, apart from *The Sailor Who Fell from Grace with the Sea* by my cat's namesake, and an anthology of haiku that I was given years ago. I thought I'd start with that.

Among the haiku, I found one by Issa that was ideal for reciting to Mishima, who observed me from his comfortable position on the couch.

Arise from sleep, old cat,
And with great yawns and stretchings,
Amble out for love.

Mishima thumped his tail a couple of times but didn't move. He was probably still too young to amble out for love. Then I read him a traditional Japanese song, which I thought was especially tender:

232

Two things will never change,
not today or any other day,
for they have been here since time began:
the water's flow
and the strange, sweet nature of love.

This was certainly a good definition of love, because if it wasn't strange I'd never have managed to get Gabriela to agree to see me the following day.

I was wildly happy and full of energy. Someone once said that, when you fall in love, you're not really in love with the person but with life through that person. This was happening to me.

The problem was that I didn't know how long I'd be able to contain my feelings. Despite the rules I set for myself, I wanted to confess my love every time I was with her, which would have been totally counterproductive. For the moment, she'd given me only her friendship, and I had to cling to that, come what may. That didn't stop me from rehearsing my crazy declarations of love in private.

A book from Titus's shelves turned out to be the perfect source of inspiration for this. It's called *10,000 Ways to Say I Love You.*

It's hard to believe there could be so many variations on the phrase, but the author, a guy named Godek, had set out to make it into the *Guinness World Records* with his project. Some of his more extravagant suggestions include suggestions like:

Writing "I love you" on your teeth (one letter per tooth) with a pen that's not toxic and flashing a big smile so your beloved can read it.

A flyer campaign in your neighborhood with your photo, your beloved's name, and the message, "Love me!"

Saying it over the phone in Morse code by tapping a glass with a spoon.

Making a gift of yourself, nicely wrapped up and delivered by friends to the beloved's home on his or her birthday.

Making and sharing a pizza on which the topping forms a big heart.

Closing your eyes to be kissed after writing "I love you" on your eyelids.

Who Is Lobsang Rampa?

Because of my great mood and the prospect of a week off—until the second semester started—I received Valdemar warmly that night and was even enthusiastic about engaging in conversation with him.

As if to counteract my energy, this time he was gloomy and dejected. He gave the impression of being tormented or threatened by messages from his persecutors. With the light switched off, he smoked a whole cigarette before deciding to speak. Meanwhile, I'd poured myself a glass of wine and was studying his movements, or those of his shadow, with an anthropologist's curiosity.

Valdemar, who had placed his ever-present backpack on the floor, began the night's chat with a question to himself.

"Who was Lobsang Rampa? Whatever the case, he wasn't who we thought he was. Millions of people who read *The Third Eye* were convinced he was a Tibetan lama who'd attained the supernatural powers he describes in his book. Although it was a best seller for decades, no television channel ever managed to interview him. This raised his profile even further, because people love mystery. His trump card was the fact that nobody knew what he looked like. That's why, last century, people preferred what they believed to be the dark side of the moon before it was photographed. Reality, or what we take to be reality, has never been of any interest to most people."

"So, who is Lobsang Rampa?"

"Nobody. That's the problem. Lobsang Rampa doesn't exist as such. After he'd conned the whole world with the lama story, some journalists from the *Times* discovered that he was a plumber whose real name was Cyril Henry Hoskin. He'd never been to Tibet. The most surprising thing is that people didn't seem to be put off by that, because the book kept selling. What sort of world do we live in? Now do you understand why I have nostalgia for the future?"

"I think that some people can't make their real identity public because nobody would accept it." I was surprised to find myself defending the Francis Amalfis of this world.

"What do you mean by that?"

"The author might have wanted to use his real name, but nobody would have taken any notice, starting with the publisher. The world wanted Lobsang Rampa, not Cyril Henry Hoskin."

"Are you trying to tell me that it's not necessary to practice what you preach? That you can go around thinking one thing, saying another, and doing something else? Is that what you believe?"

"I'm only saying we're human beings. It wouldn't be just to ask more of Lobsang Rampa than I'd ask of myself."

Valdemar took a deep drag. He exhaled slowly.

"I've come to the conclusion that, not only do we live in a fake world, but it's impossible to share any experience."

"What makes you think that?"

"I'll give you an example to explain what I mean. Imagine that I want to go off on a long journey, and I don't know when I'll be back. You come with me to the railway station to say good-bye. If after that we stay in touch by e-mail or phone, and we both reminisce about that farewell, it will be pure self-deception."

"Why?"

"Because we're not talking about the same thing, however much we want to believe we are. Your memory is different from mine and could even be the complete opposite. You remember a man getting on a train, moving away into the distance, and waving good-bye out of a window. I, however, remember a man standing still on a platform, getting smaller and smaller. That's the only thing we can share: the sensation that the other person is getting smaller. This is true of our emotional lives too. Experience can never be shared. It's served in separate packets."

"Do you want a glass of wine? I guess we'll be talking for a while yet."

Just then, Mishima started racing up and down the hallway, as if he realized that the night was going to be important somehow and that he needed to stay fit and alert.

The Empty Backpack

When I woke up in my chair it took me quite a while to figure out where I was, as if I'd had a grand mal absence. The early-morning light bounced off two empty wine bottles and another that was almost full.

Judging by the hangover that made me fear my head was going to explode, we must have been drinking and talking nonstop until I'd dropped off to sleep. Valdemar must have staggered off to the upstairs apartment but had left his backpack lying on the floor.

I felt that tidying up was an even more urgent task than trying to sort myself out, so I collected the bottles and emptied the ashtray, which was full of half-smoked cigarettes. When I picked up the backpack I noticed that it was very light. I opened the zipper and saw that it was empty.

That was surprising because Valdemar carried his manuscript around in it. I hadn't seen him open it once the previous night. How could it be empty now? The only possible answer was that he'd come down with an empty backpack, just as I'd found it. But why would anyone carry around a backpack with nothing inside it? Unless he'd planned to take something away in it. But this couldn't have been the case, since the backpack was still lying there, empty.

Two aspirin and a cold shower later, my hangover had been reduced to a state of feeling slightly out of sorts. I forced myself to eat a couple of slices of bread with cheese.

It must have been about ten when I went out, still feeling woozy. I had two hours to recover before meeting Gabriela, who had the morning off.

I should have thought about this before I started drinking.

The fresh air felt like soothing balm on my skin.

Choosing a Novel

This time we'd arranged to meet in the café at La Central, the biggest bookshop in El Raval. Since I got there an hour early, I decided to browse in the foreign-literature section.

I started leafing through a book called *Death and the Penguin* by the popular Ukrainian writer Andrey Kurkov. It's about loneliness and life in post-Soviet Ukraine. Viktor, a struggling writer, adopts a penguin after the Kiev zoo gives away its animals when it can no longer feed them. After embarking on a series of adventures together in Kiev, they get embroiled in a complicated situation.

Seduced by this find, I decided I'd take the penguin and its protector home with me. As I was going to pay for the book, I thought that if I had a new novel, then Gabriela should have one too. But which? It's not easy to guess the tastes of someone you barely know, even if she's read Somerset Maugham and Graham Greene.

In such cases, there's a surefire solution, however, which is to give something you'd like yourself. But you have to be careful about your choice, because the title can say a lot about your intentions toward that person. It's not the same thing to give a woman a book called *Tell*

Me You Love Me Even If It's a Lie as it is to give *Memoirs of a Bitch*.

I went and asked one of the assistants if they had *The Flaw* by Antonis Samarakis. It looks like a crime novel at first, but in the end you realize that it's also the story of a friendship. I remember having tears in my eyes when I finished it, which doesn't happen to me very often. Yes, that was a good choice.

The Flaw

When Gabriela came into the bookshop café, I was having a cup of the house special, a blend called Monk's Tea, which seemed most adequate for the image of self-restraint I was trying to convey.

She asked for the same tea as I had. While they were making it behind the bar, I placed the book I'd chosen for her on the table.

"What's that?" She was surprised.

"Since we're in a bookshop, it must be a book." I was trying to be funny.

"How did you know it's my birthday today? Have you hired a private detective?"

I was upset by her suspicion, although the amazing coincidence quickly made me forget my indignation. Whatever the case, I needed to be a bit cool and distant, so I said, "I didn't know. Happy birthday! Actually, I'm like the Mad Hatter and the March Hare because I'm into unbirthdays."

"So it really is a coincidence," she marveled.

"Aren't you going to open it?" I asked impatiently.

Her long fingers tore the paper off, as if she were trying to free the book from a shroud. When *The Flaw* emerged, she looked at it lying on the table but didn't touch it, except for a long lock of hair that fell onto it, covering the author's name.

"I don't know this one," she said.

"That's why I'm giving it to you. It's one of my favorite novels."

I shouldn't have done that. I've put unnecessary pressure on her with this gift. Now she'll think she has to respond in some way.

"Thank you," she said, putting the book in the pocket of her woolen overcoat.

I had to salvage the situation as soon as possible, so I drained my teacup and suggested, "Shall we go? Today's my first day off, and I'd love to go for a walk."

Gabriela nodded and, with a vacant expression, got up, leaving her cup still full on the table. It was only then that I noticed that she hadn't touched it. I definitely couldn't have been more inept.

Leaving the bookshop, we walked along the street leading to the Plaça dels Àngels. There's an old building there and a couple of tall, thin palm trees that I've always liked, but that morning they looked like two poor creatures being flayed by the wind—just like Gabriela and me.

"What's Osaka like?" I asked, hoping to break the silence that had set in between us.

"They call it the Venice of Japan because it

244

has so many canals. But it's nothing like Venice. It's a modern city with lots of students."

She lapsed into silence again. I didn't ask any more questions, and she didn't seem willing to take the initiative, as on our last date. What was going on?

As I often do in desperate situations, I chose precisely that moment to do something very rash. When we walked into the large square, I took her hand in mine. Astonishingly, she didn't reject it or say anything. She didn't even stop walking, despite this new turn of events. We just kept going toward the center of the square, which was full of skaters and musicians.

I was holding her cold, soft hand, but she wasn't really holding mine. Instead of closing hers a little around mine to show she was responding to my move, it was hanging there limply, like a creature without a will of its own.

"Do you mind my holding your hand?"

"I don't mind. The problem is what it means to you."

After that dig, I let go of her hand. It fell to her side, heavy as lead, like a bird shot down by a bullet. That was the point of no return, and it was entirely my fault because I hadn't been patient enough or had sufficient control over myself to win her friendship and trust little by little.

She had very clearly grasped my intentions, and now I'd lost everything. It was too late for the cautious, stealthy approach decreed by the golden laws of seduction.

With my whole project ruined, I didn't have it in me to keep hanging on to false hopes.

"Gabriela, I'm sorry for having hassled you now and over the past week. I'm no good at flirting. Let me be honest with you: I don't think we can ever be friends."

"We can't?" She was shocked.

"It'd be wonderful to be your friend, because it's a privilege to spend time with you. But I love you too much to keep pretending. Gabriela, walk away now or I'll have to kiss you."

Once the words were out, I was overwhelmed by a dizzying need to flee and rushed off without waiting for her reaction. My head was spinning as I scurried away from the square. I felt like the most ridiculous man in the world because, having made my threat, I was the one who'd run away.

From the Heights

I spent the rest of the day wandering around the city like a man possessed, in the hope that the exhaustion would make me forget what had just happened. I escaped from El Raval into the Sant Antoni neighborhood and then walked up through L'Esquerra de l'Eixample.

When I reached Avinguda Diagonal—which has traditionally separated the rich from the rest of Barcelona—I kept going north, impelled by some mysterious urge. I knew that as soon as I got home the whole world would collapse on my head, so I decided to continue on my expedition until I was completely worn out.

On a whim, I decided to stop walking in a straight line, so I turned into Carrer Muntaner and kept climbing up toward the mountain. My feet were boiling hot when the sun reached its zenith. Walking past schoolchildren, executives, and well-to-do retirees, I understood that I'd have to keep walking until I'd left every last remnant of the city behind me. Only then would I stop.

I got to Plaça de la Bonanova and turned left, looking for a street that would let me continue my mad ascent. I found one that ran alongside a prestigious business school and kept going up the slope without looking back.

After climbing for twenty minutes, I reached the point where the blocks of luxury apartments gave way to large and small mansions. After that, a few run-down villas. Finally, there was only the forest.

Tired after my long walk, I sat down under a stand of pines that, rearranged by gravity, were leaning at odd angles. For the first time I managed to calm down more or less. It was a relief to have the city at my feet and to know that, even if just for a few minutes, I wasn't part of it.

From my lofty vantage point all desires and aspirations seemed insignificant. It was like watching the frenzied activity of an anthill.

While I filled my lungs with resin-scented air, I could see the sun's orb sinking slowly and inexorably down toward the horizon. A little bit of common sense began to emerge from the calm that had settled inside me.

I've ruined this girl's birthday. I should really just go home and try not to crash into the furniture.

V

One Day in a Life

The Disappearance

I was much calmer when I walked down the mountain and finally got home with the night sky over my head, unaware that the weirdest twenty-four hours of my life still lay in store for me.

I could have gone to see a film in order to distract myself from my worries, but I was too tired to concentrate on a movie. The best option was probably to go to bed and forget about my situation.

As I climbed the stairs, I was convinced that Gabriela would have left a message on my answering machine. Either she'd ask if I was OK—which would be very kind of her—or she'd take me to task for my behavior and tell me to not bother her anymore.

At least she was very close to home. I had to climb a mountain to find myself again. I turned the key in my door.

There was no message. That hurt. Didn't she care about my suffering?

I took a shower, and by the time I came out I was quite resigned.

I got into my pajamas and, since I wasn't hungry, I started wandering around the apartment, tidying up here and there as Mishima kept an eye on me. Coming across Valdemar's backpack for a second time made me uneasy.

How come he hadn't tried to come and get it? What if he'd been so drunk he'd hit his head and was lying there upstairs, badly injured?

There was only one way to find out. In my pajamas and slippers I went upstairs and rang the bell a few times. Its familiar sound was all I heard. Nothing else.

It took me quite a while to notice—after ringing the bell for the third time—that the door wasn't closed but had been left slightly ajar. Even more worried, I pushed it open, certain I was going to find the remnants of some awful catastrophe.

However, when I turned on the light, everything looked impeccable, which seemed at odds with the open door. The keys were hanging from the lock on the inside. I put them in my pocket before closing the door and continuing my investigation.

The lemon-scented air suggested that the floor had just been mopped. The living room was clean and tidy, and the computer sat on its table, where not a single speck of dust was visible. I looked in the direction of the kitchen, which, like mine, had a window opening onto the outside. Then I started feeling really alarmed.

There, in the middle of the kitchen, was a large

telescope mounted on a tripod, one end poking out of the window and up to the sky.

I left the kitchen without touching anything and searched the entire place, calling Valdemar and checking every room, including the closets. Then I remembered the metal box he'd brought the first night. Without a doubt it had contained the telescope. He wouldn't have gone away leaving that behind him unless something unexpected had forced him to flee.

The same sixth sense that had alerted me when I saw the empty backpack told me that Valdemar wouldn't be coming back. I inspected the apartment once more, only to discover that everything was in its place, even the cigarettes. Only the manuscript was missing. It was very strange.

I went back to the kitchen feeling bewildered. There was a handwritten note tucked under a saucer that I'd missed the first time I'd looked. The message was both simple and disturbing:

I'VE LEFT. WILL I BE BACK?

With a heavy heart and a guilty conscience because I'd been so remiss, I looked through the eyepiece to see if the stars might offer me some clue as to Valdemar's whereabouts. As if it had prior knowledge of the exact moment of my arrival, the telescope was focused on the full moon.

I don't know how long I remained there, mesmerized, exploring the craters and dark seas that may have once held water. I missed Valdemar but was comforted by the thought that he'd gotten there somehow. I imagined that, right then, he was looking at me from some crater through a powerful telescope that had been left behind by the *Apollo 17* astronauts.

The Night of the End of the World

It was midnight. Perturbed by what had just happened, I got dressed again and went out to walk through the streets and get some fresh air.

From the pavement I looked up at the two top floors of my side of the building. After recent events it had turned into a shadowy mausoleum, and I'd decided to run away before I was sealed inside forever. I didn't want to share the same fate as the man from Tokyo.

Just above my head, a gigantic moon shed an eerie light over the city.

I was fascinated by the sight. I didn't remember ever having seen the moon so close. It was as if it was only half its usual distance away. What if it was heading toward us because of some nasty trick of gravity? Then it would keep getting bigger and bigger until it crashed into earth. The end of the world was nigh.

Was there some connection with Valdemar's disappearance?

There was no way I could stay at home. If this was the night of the end of the world, I wasn't going to spend it in bed.

Maybe it was due to the proximity of the moon, but that February night was particularly warm.

My legs were aching after the afternoon's urban marathon, but I was high on adrenaline, so I walked to the city center with my eyes wide open.

I was certain that Valdemar's flight was only the prelude to something momentous and inevitable. Instinct told me that this was going to be an eventful night, culminating in the moon's collision with the earth. The final kiss of a love affair that had lasted 4,600 million years.

The strangest thing was that I wasn't afraid. I accepted the catastrophe as a suitable end to my wretched existence.

As I walked down Passeig de Gràcia, I could see that a lot of people had the same idea as me. It was almost one in the morning, yet the street was packed.

Nobody seemed scared. More than anything, people seemed fascinated and kept flashing their digital cameras to capture the phenomenon. How could they be in such a good mood watching the disaster that was about to hit them?

Tired of dodging the crowds of people who kept colliding with one another because they were staring at the sky, I turned onto Gran Via to walk down the last stretch of Carrer Balmes. I hadn't intended to go to the bar at the crossroads, but there I was, standing right outside it. The blind was halfway down, but the light was on. I thought that if Valdemar was anywhere in this world, he'd have to be inside.

After weeks of not going there, it seemed like a good spot to see in the end of the world. I ducked under the metal blind and entered the bar.

17 Minutes

When I popped up from behind the half-lowered blind, the waiter looked at me with ill-concealed annoyance. Convinced that the end of the world gave me total impunity, I leaned against the bar and asked for a glass of wine.

"We're closed, but since you're a regular I'll serve you," he said, uncorking a new bottle.

After he'd poured my wine, he disappeared into the kitchen, from which I could hear the sounds of a radio news program.

Alone at the bar, I sipped my wine and glanced at the day's newspaper. On the front page there was a big photo of the moon hanging low over the rooftops of Barcelona. Perhaps they'd announced the end of the world and I hadn't heard the news. Was I so cut off from everything?

Before I could read the article, a familiar figure entered the bar. It was the man in black, the red-head, the seventeen-minute fellow. The night was starting to get interesting.

"We're closed," the waiter shouted from the kitchen.

I stood up for him. "He's a regular."

Now that my heart was broken, I realized that there were only two things I wanted to do before the end came: read the article and time the man in black for the third and last time.

The waiter cursed out loud before leaving his bunker to get him a beer.

"You've got fifteen minutes and then I'm closing," he informed us.

"Can't you give us a bit more time?" I asked, thinking of the magic number.

He shot me a withering look, then vanished again and turned up the radio, which was now airing a scientific debate. Was Valdemar among the experts?

I checked my watch. It was ten past one. I kept an eye on the minute hand and read the newspaper at the same time.

WINTER MOON ILLUSION: scientists fail to come to any agreement as to the causes of the phenomenon.

Agencies. A NASA communiqué states that the moon will appear to be twice its usual size tonight. This is a purely optical phenomenon known as the "moon illusion" or, in more technical terms, the "apparent distance theory."

Although the exact causes of this effect—usually a summer occurrence, which makes today's phenomenon so exceptional—are as yet unknown, it would seem that the illusion is created by the convergence of rays of light from the moon, which appears much larger to observers when it is near the horizon.

This optical illusion results from the way in which the moon is perceived by the naked eye. It does not occur with cameras. To demonstrate this, NASA suggests an interesting experiment: isolate the moon by looking at it through a cutout circle or a tube. Once the reference points of its surroundings are thus eliminated, the magical effect disappears.

Annoyed, I closed the newspaper. What I had almost looked forward to turned out to be an illusion.

We'll have to wait a bit longer for the end of the world. I checked my watch: twenty-seven past one. Set in motion by some invisible mechanism, the redhead left a coin on the bar and agilely ducked underneath the blind to emerge on the other side.

I felt an overwhelming urge to follow him. I was too tired to resist the impulse.

Even though it was late, I went after him. The huge, ghostly moon hovered over our heads.

Elevator Bar

The man in black strode across Carrer Pelai and kept going down Portal de l'Àngel, after which he turned left, heading for the cathedral.

I followed fairly close behind, like a detective hoping for a breakthrough in order to solve a case. Actually, I had embarked on this pursuit in order to ward off the pain of having lost Gabriela. All good detectives have something in their past they want to forget about.

The seventeen-minute man reached the cathedral. Now the moon looked like a gigantic, milk-colored fruit impaled on its highest spire. Then he took one of the side alleys, Carrer del Bisbe, which passes beneath a neo-Gothic bridge linking two old buildings.

The street was deserted, so I lagged a little farther behind, trying to make sure that my shoes made no sound on the ancient cobblestones. He, too, slowed down to light a cigarette, staring at the sky as he did so.

We crossed the Plaça de Sant Jaume and continued along one of the streets leading to the port, although the enigmatic redhead soon turned off to the left into Carrer Bellafilla. He paused for a moment outside a well-lit door before going inside.

Once he'd entered his lair, I stopped, just a few steps away from what turned out to be the door of a cocktail bar called L'Ascensor. True to its name, the entrance was an old mahogany elevator with sliding doors. It still had its original early-twentieth-century buttons.

In that old, out-of-place elevator, wondering what to do next, I remembered the final scene of the film *Angel Heart*, in which Mickey Rourke descends into the bowels of hell in an elevator.

The sliding door opened onto a small bar with mirrors and marble tables. Still hesitating, I went inside. All the tables were occupied by groups of young people cheerfully downing their drinks in that fin de siècle atmosphere.

I stayed close to the bar, not sure what to do. I wasn't Mickey Rourke, and anyway I was very tired.

As often happens in such moments of indecision, someone else took the initiative. The black-clad redhead suddenly got up from his table—which he was sharing with two very good-looking women—and came over to me, with a grim expression on his face.

His companions, who couldn't have been much over twenty, observed the scene, somewhere between amused and expectant. I think one of them, a girl with extraordinarily blue eyes, said something along the lines of "Let him be."

Leaning against the bar, I had no idea how I

was supposed to deal with this situation and stop it from turning into an undignified fracas. Before I could decide what to do, the redhead asked, politely but firmly, "Were you following me?"

The only answer I could come up with—and which was not really Hollywood material—was "Yes."

"Would you care to tell me why?"

"I'm helping a friend with a study in urban anthropology, and we're looking at the habits of bar-goers, especially people who stick to some kind of predetermined ritual like yourself."

He stood there with his arms crossed, studying me as if waiting for the evidence to be presented before pronouncing his verdict. Yet a faint smile told me that the man was not looking for trouble and only having a bit of fun at my expense.

Feigning indignation, he asked, "What makes you think I'm one of your bar creatures?"

"We're regulars at the same bar. In fact, thanks to my earlier intervention you were able to have your beer . . . in seventeen minutes."

That last comment seemed to mollify him, since he loosened up, patted my shoulder, and said, "Come and sit with us. Let's have a drink."

Seeing us coming over, one of the girls, a brunette with an angular face, stood up and said to me, "Here, take my chair. I've got to get up in five hours."

Before I could respond, I was sitting between

the blue-eyed girl and the redhead, who called the waiter over by snapping his fingers. The girl then put the icing on the cake of this bizarre gathering.

"Rubén," she said, "this is Samuel de Juan."

I was flabbergasted. It's always awkward when someone you don't know recognizes you. I didn't want to say something embarrassing like "Who are you?" so I waited for some kind of clue to put me on the right track.

The girl continued, smiling, "He's my contemporary literature lecturer. We'll have to get him drunk so he does something crazy, and then he'll have to give me a good mark to buy my silence."

Then the penny dropped. This was Miss Know-It-All, Round-Specs. Since she wasn't wearing her glasses that night, I hadn't recognized her. Her nearsighted deep-blue eyes gave her a fragile look, which was very different from the impression she gave in my classroom.

"That won't be necessary. You've already got it. The results will be out in a couple of days."

She must have been drinking for a while, because she threw herself at me and planted a loud kiss on my cheek. I felt suffocated and unable to hide my discomfort, but luckily the waiter came over and saved me from this tricky situation.

"Three aquavits with ice, please," said Rubén.

He was clearly a nightlife veteran, because he

was brash enough to order for the whole table without asking what anyone wanted. As if to justify his unilateral action, he leaned over and muttered to me, "To celebrate my friend's success."

Before going off to get the drinks, the waiter asked, "Do you want Line?"

"Of course!" He seemed offended.

"What's Line?" my student asked.

To which I added: "What's aquavit?"

Pleased that his choice had aroused such interest, Rubén smiled and began his lecture. "Aquavit is a Norwegian spirit. A friend of mine here introduced me to it. There are two kinds, the normal one and the *Linie* aquavit, which is much more expensive because it's aged in oak barrels then loaded onto ships sailing from Norway to Australia and back again, which means it crosses the line of the Equator twice before it's bottled. Only then can it use the official *Linie* label."

Conversation with an Engineer

Luckily, L'Ascensor closed at half past two, which meant I only had to have a couple of glasses.

"My friend lives right here, almost next door," Rubén said, his car keys in his hand. "Do you want a lift home?"

"Don't worry, thanks."

"It's no problem. It'll give us a chance to talk about urban anthropology. Don't you want to know about the seventeen minutes?"

I got a second kiss from my student, which destroyed any remnant of academic authority I might still have had, and walked with the redhead to a nearby parking lot, from which he emerged in a brand-new Saab sports car. He was clearly a man of Nordic tastes.

"I spend a lot of time in Scandinavia," he answered when I mentioned this to him. "I'm an oil-well engineer, but I'm on vacation now."

As we drove slowly up Via Laietana, he gave me a brief account of his life. He lived alone in an uptown apartment but only used it two months per year. The two girls were friends from high school.

"I don't have the time to find a girlfriend," he

informed me without my asking. "With all the coming and going, the best I can hope for is the occasional tryst."

Another loner. I'd met a lot of them since the new year.

We stopped talking for a while. I let my thoughts drift among the blurry lights of the cars coming toward us, as I brooded over my woeful behavior with Gabriela in the Plaça dels Àngels.

It seemed incredible that I'd committed this blunder earlier that day, the same day that was now coming to an end. So many things had happened since then: my flight up the mountain, Valdemar's disappearance, the moon illusion, my encounter with the redhead, and, subsequently, the blue-eyed student.

Even so, I suspected that I hadn't reached the end of the story. A couple more surprises surely still lay in store for me in this crazy dash from one outlandish episode to another. But nothing could fill the void left by my debacle with Gabriela.

The engineer pulled me out of my well of sorrows.

"When I'm in Barcelona, I often go to the bar at the crossroads. It's a stop on my way to buy books in the city center."

"But why do you always stay for seventeen minutes?"

"It's a favor I do for you."

He lit a cigarette and offered me one, which I rejected, thinking he was just as loony as Valdemar.

"I'm also observant. One day at lunchtime, I was sitting outside and noticed the bearded guy writing down the exact time each customer spent in the bar in his notebook, so I decided that from then on I'd always stay there for seventeen minutes. It was a kind of game. Then I saw that you were timing me too, so I kept doing it because I didn't want to disappoint you."

I leaned my head against the back of the leather seat and said, "This relationship that has sprung up between you and us is like the one between quantum physics and particles. You were there for seventeen minutes because that's what we wanted to see."

"Right. As I said, I was doing you a favor."

The car stopped in front of my door and the engineer said good-bye, patting me on the shoulder as if I were some kind of silly teenager, though I was ten years older than him.

"As far as I'm concerned, you can break your routine at the bar," I said as we parted. "Have a second beer next time."

"I'll have one with you two," he said, and drove off.

Death Misses the Train

I was dead on my feet when I got back to my place in the small hours of the morning. I flopped on my bed and fell asleep.

However, before seven that morning my slumber was interrupted when the doorbell rang with long, insistent blasts. An emergency. The abruptness of my awakening enabled me to hang on to the last scene of the dream I was having: Valdemar was walking along the hallway of my apartment with the manuscript in his hand, following Mishima, who was leading him somewhere.

Another salvo from the doorbell put an end to my recollection, so I didn't get a chance to remember where Mishima had taken Valdemar.

It's as if he's gone back to the moon. I shot out of bed still half asleep.

When I answered on the intercom I got the shock of my life, because the person on the other end wasn't the one I had imagined. An unexpected voice said, "Samuel . . ."

Had my ears deceived me? That couldn't be Titus down there on the street! Yet it sounded like his voice. I clasped the handset to my ear. Yes, it was Titus, and he was clearly getting impatient, because he shouted, "Open up, will you! And come down and help me!"

Like a kid seeing his father again on his return from a long journey, I flew downstairs and flung myself into Titus's arms. He was beside himself with joy but pretended to be annoyed.

"You told me you were dying," I reminded him.

"It was the only way to get you to listen to me. Anyway, I didn't say anything that wasn't true. We all start dying the day we're born, but there are lots of rebirths along the way."

I was delighted. "So are you cured?"

"No one's ever cured of anything, least of all at my age. But let's just say death missed the train and will turn up some other day."

Revelations

I immediately understood that this wasn't the end of the story. Somehow Valdemar had left so that Titus could come back, even though they didn't know one another. And that was just the tip of the iceberg.

Now I had to explain a lot of things, like why there was a telescope in his kitchen. Yet Titus didn't seem very interested, because when I pointed at it he merely said, "Yes, I can see that it's a telescope. I'm not blind, you know."

"Aren't you surprised to find it here?"

"Valdemar asked me if he could set it up in there, and I said yes. So let's leave it there for now."

I didn't understand anything anymore.

"What do you mean he asked you if he could? How come? Do you know him?"

"We've been speaking almost every day since the first time I called from the hospital and he answered the phone."

Disconcerted, I wondered why, if he was in hiding, Valdemar would have answered a stranger's phone. The only reasonable explanation was that he must have thought I was calling him from downstairs.

"He gave me a brief account of his situation

and asked me not to get angry with you for letting him stay at my place. I told him he could stay as long as he needed."

"Why didn't you tell me?"

"I thought you had enough on your plate. I phoned my apartment thinking I'd find you there hard at work. But thanks to Valdemar I discovered that you hadn't made any progress on the book."

"He told you that?" I was mortified.

"Yes, but he was trying to make excuses for you. He said you were going through a rough patch, even though you were pretending everything was fine. This man knows a lot more than he lets on."

"Where is he now?"

"How should I know? Yesterday I told him that I was coming home this morning but that he could stay on. Valdemar's a good fellow. He'd do anything to avoid being a nuisance."

Serenitas

After Titus's revelations, I went home determined to keep a level head. In other words, I'd deal with each new calamity as it happened, without too much worrying beforehand.

An article about Mendelssohn in a magazine I subscribed to made me want to listen to Barenboim's version of *Songs without Words* again, after days of feeling I couldn't bear to hear it.

Lying on my couch, I started reading a short essay on the composer, written by someone named Andrés Sánchez Pascual. I thought it was excellent. This is how he defines Mendelssohn's music:

> The pleasure it gives is not facile, trifling or crude, but is a much subtler form of delight, one that is full of melancholy; this feeling may perhaps be most precisely expressed by the Latin word *serenitas*.

As the first notes of the second gondolier started in the background, I came upon a curious fact about *Songs without Words*. In 1842, a relative of Mendelssohn's wife asked him what the purpose of these short pieces was, and he answered by letter:

So much is spoken about music and so little is said. For my part I do not believe that words suffice for such a task, and if they did I would no longer make any music. . . . The thoughts that are expressed to me by the music I love are not too vague to put into words but, on the contrary, too precise.

The Moon's Damp Cage

Serenitas fell by the wayside when my doorbell rang, this time from the landing. Judging by the racket, it could only have been Titus on the other side, bearing news.

I invited him in. The old man affectionately patted my back, which was most unusual for him. He was carrying a folder with elastic bands around it.

"Does the music bother you?" I asked, turning down the volume.

"What bothers me is that you're so modest."

"Why do you say that?"

I sat down on the couch.

Titus also took a seat and said, "*A Short Course in Everyday Magic* is magnificent. Congratulations. I'll send it to the publisher tomorrow. I'll pay you the entire fee and won't take no for an answer."

"But . . . what on earth are you talking about? I don't recall writing more than fifteen pages."

"Well, by my count it's a hundred and twenty-eight." He opened the folder, which was full of printed pages. "Not only are you modest but you're a liar too, it would appear."

"Let me see," I asked, grabbing the folder to make sure he wasn't pulling my leg.

Quickly flipping through the pages, I was baffled to see that somehow, inexplicably, the work was not only finished but beautifully written. Each one of the seven chapters—including "Love in Lowercase"—was almost twenty pages long and full of inspirational passages. The anthology concluded with a traditional Celtic poem. The last two lines read:

You can call up the spirits of the night,
And cage in a puddle the moon and its light.

Completely nonplussed, I handed it back to him and said, "Pay Valdemar, if you can find him. This is his work, of course."

I spent the rest of the afternoon telling Titus about how I'd met Valdemar at the bar, his accident in Patagonia, the mysterious people on the platform, his early-morning arrival at my place, and our late-night conversations.

Titus listened, nodding his head but without paying much attention, as if he already knew most of the details. However, when I got to our drinking session and the empty backpack and the dream from which he, Titus, had awakened me, he suddenly became interested.

"So in your dream Valdemar was holding the manuscript in his hand when he was following the cat?"

"Yes," I said, looking at Mishima, who was happily rolling around on the rug. "Strange, isn't it?"

Titus burst out laughing. "What's strange is how thick you are. I'm surprised you can't understand such a clear message. In your dream, the cat was showing you the hiding place of Valdemar's manuscript. That's all that's left of him and his research now. So it's our duty to find it and keep it safe."

"Hiding place!" I repeated. "That's it! Every time Mishima's had to have an injection he disappears into a hiding place that I've never been able to find."

"If there's room for a cat, there's room for a—" Titus began.

"Manuscript!" I finished. "The problem is I've never been able to find out where he goes."

"Let him show us himself," Titus suggested. "You only need to phone the vet. I'll follow him."

It was such a simple, obvious idea that it was hard to believe it would actually work, but I did what he suggested. I picked up the phone and dialed the number of the clinic. A few seconds later, I heard Meritxell's voice on the other end of the line.

"Good afternoon. I have a cat named Mishima, and he's due for vaccination," I said, emphasizing the words "Mishima" and "vaccination."

From the corner of my eye, I could see Mishima

get up, stretch, and sneak off down the hallway.

"Is this some kind of joke or have you been spending too much time with that neighbor of yours?"

"I'll explain later," I said, as quietly as I could. I hung up and went to join Titus's expedition.

He was standing next to the door of the closet in which I kept the clothes I wasn't using. He put his index finger to his lips.

"He's in there," he mouthed.

We looked at each other as if waiting for instructions. What now? In the end I decided to open the closet door, which was ajar, to reveal the great mystery.

At first we could see only old jackets and trousers and a dusty shoebox on the top shelf. I removed the box, thinking that Mishima could be hiding inside, but it turned out to be empty. To my surprise, however, it had concealed a hole in the wall.

There he was. Mishima's eyes were as round as saucers. He was astonished that we'd found his hideout. He would have to find another one now.

I tried to grab him, but he sprang down gracefully and dashed along the hallway. The manuscript was there.

I handed it to Titus, and he received it like a precious gift. Pink with emotion, he said, "Since Valdemar has been living in my apartment, let me keep the manuscript. And I might need the telescope to check a few things."

"All yours."

"Come up tonight, if you like, so we can study it together. It might give us a clue as to his whereabouts. There are lots of things that you still don't know about him."

The Poet's Rose

As soon as Titus had left, I went to lie down on my bed, hoping that a quick nap might help me digest what had happened.

It was six in the evening and my bedroom was already dark. Mishima was miffed because we'd tricked him—although our victory was only temporary—and didn't join me this time.

I tried to sleep for an hour, floating between waking and sleeping, the kind of limbo where you leave your body behind and your thoughts wander without coming up with anything in particular.

This neutral, meditative state was suddenly interrupted by the sound of the bedroom door slowly opening. A meow in the darkness told me that Mishima was no longer angry and wanted my attention.

I got out of the bed, imagining that he wanted food or water or that the litter box needed cleaning. He was very demanding in that regard. Yet, when I checked, I could see that everything was in perfect order. So why had he gotten me out of bed?

I puttered around in the kitchen, trying to decide whether to make myself some coffee or not. There was a sheet of paper on the floor. It must have dropped out of Titus's—or, technically speaking, Francis Amalfi's—folder.

I picked it up and sat on the couch to read it, expecting yet another revelation.

It was from the "Heart in the Hand" section and took the form of a supposedly true story about the young Rainer Maria Rilke's first stay in Paris.

He used to walk—accompanied by a girl— through a square where a woman went to beg. She always sat in the same place, without looking at the passersby, without asking for their charity, and without ever showing gratitude when someone gave her something. Although his friend often gave her a coin, Rilke never gave her anything.

One day the young woman asked him why, and he said, "It's her heart that needs a gift, not her hand."

A few days later, Rilke placed a rose in the woman's cracked and leathery palm. Then something surprising happened. She looked up and, after effusively covering his hand with kisses, stood up and left the square, waving the rose around. Her spot was unoccupied for a whole week, after which she came back to reclaim it.

"But what has she been living on all these days if she hasn't been begging in the square?" the girl asked.

"The rose," Rilke replied.

Closing the Circle

I didn't bother returning the missing page to Titus. Instead I went downstairs, planning to walk to the city center.

It was one of those decisions that only make sense long after you've made them. Somehow I'd accepted that the leitmotif for the day was "Anything can happen," so I wanted to get to the music shop before it closed.

Titus's return, Valdemar's disappearance, and the discovery of his manuscript had unleashed so many doubts that I was determined to sort out at least one thing, and this depended on me and me alone. I'd offended Gabriela and had to apologize. It was the only way to put an end to the whole sorry affair.

This time, I needed no pretext. I'd just walk into the music shop, say I was sorry for my stupid behavior, and wish her luck. If I could leave it at that, order would be restored. Sooner or later, love's wounds would heal and I'd eventually go back to my quiet, solitary existence. Recent events heralded more troubles ahead, and I was going to need all my strength to deal with them.

I got there just in time to see Gabriela lowering the metal blind. I stopped some three yards away from her, careful not to invade her space. Before she saw me, I mustered the whole world's supply of *serenitas* and rehearsed the words of the apology I'd prepared in advance.

However, when she turned and glared at me with those almond-shaped eyes, I couldn't speak. I was trying to come up with a briefer version of my expression of regret, but she beat me to it.

"I've been trying to call you since yesterday, but your phone's busy all the time. Why do you act like this? I was worried about you."

After my initial shock, I remembered that I'd disconnected my phone and answering machine two days earlier, for the afternoon snack with Meritxell. I had forgotten to plug them in again. Only someone who never gets phone calls would be capable of such an oversight.

"Never mind," she said when I didn't answer, "the most important thing is that you're OK. I was afraid you'd done something crazy."

"Well, I did," I confessed as we walked down La Rambla. "I walked right across Barcelona and up to the forest on Mount Tibidabo."

"What did you do then?"

"I walked back down."

She laughed. "Well, that's quite a trek!"

We walked along in silence—as far as this is possible on the most crowded street in the world. What on earth were we doing there? Was there no better place to walk?

As if answering my question, Gabriela took my hand and guided me to the pavement on one side. Now I was the one being led along like a zombie as she gently squeezed my fingers, like a little girl who wants to show her father something she's just discovered.

We went through a great stone portal leading into an art bookshop, where a poster informed us that there was an exhibition on Frida Kahlo upstairs. It showed her last painting, which she'd completed shortly before her painful death. It was a still life with watermelons. One of them was cut in half, with the following words carved into its pulp: "*VIVA LA VIDA.*" Long live life.

"Do you want to see the exhibition?" I asked, closing my hand around hers.

"I want to show you something else," she said, tugging me toward the back of the premises and then off to the right and down a dark, damp passageway, in which we had to stoop in order to move forward.

All at once, with Gabriela at my side, I was under the same staircase where we'd met thirty years earlier.

How had we gotten there? The old mansion had been transformed into an exhibition space, so I hadn't recognized it at first. Then again, I hadn't been back there since I was a small boy, so it had seemed bigger in my memory.

Gabriela flashed me a mischievous look, which

made me wonder: had she remembered the same episode as I had, but pretended otherwise the whole time? Or had she relived the experience in a dream, in the same way I'd had my revelation about the manuscript?

"Close your eyes," she murmured from the shadows, bringing her face closer to mine.

I did as I was told and, one second later, felt an almost imperceptible fluttering on my cheek. The circle was closed.

Opening my eyes, I was afraid that I'd be awakening from a dream. Yet Gabriela was still there, smiling with a challenging expression on her face.

I said, "I suppose the story ends here."

"On the contrary, this is where it begins." Her lips moved slowly toward mine, like planets condemned by gravity to collide.

FRANCESC MIRALLES is an award-winning author who has written a number of bestselling books. Born in Barcelona, he studied journalism, English literature, and German, and has worked as an editor, a translator, a ghostwriter, and a musician. *Love in Lowercase* has been translated into twenty languages.

Center Point Large Print
600 Brooks Road / PO Box 1
Thorndike, ME 04986-0001 USA

(207) 568-3717

US & Canada:
1 800 929-9108
www.centerpointlargeprint.com